TO WAGE WAR
(current days)

A novel

Rose Staine

Playlist

i. "Helium"- Sia
ii. "Somebody to Love"- One Republic
iii. "Dancing On My Own"- Calum Scott
iv. "Bad Liar"- Imagine Dragons
v. "Lips are Movin"- Meghan Trainor
vi. "Hymn for the Weekend"- Coldplay
vii. "Wake me Up"- Avicii
viii. "Arcade"- Duncan Laurence
ix. "Lose Control" Teddy Swims
x. "Live your life"- T.I. & Rihanna
xi. "Part II (on the run)- Jay-Z & Beyonce
xii. "Last night"- Morgan Wallen
xiii. "Wildest dreams"- Taylor Swift
xiv. "Still falling for you"- Ellie Goulding
xv. "You broke me first"- Tate McRae
xvi. "Wolves"- Selena Gomez
xvii. "Win Again" -Nicki Minaj
xviii. "Don't let me down"- The Chainsmokers
xix. "Strangers"- Camylio
xx. "Team" - Kurt Hugo Schneider & MAYCE
xxi. "Ho Hey" The Lumineers

Trigger Warning:

The content of this book includes foul language, murder, graphic sexual content, and gory violence.

For Kamaya Ariel. Thank You for always loving me through the dark. For being the reason, I laugh so hard, I pee a little. You will always be enough.

PROLOGUE

    The mother, a fierce but fair leader. Chosen by the people to lead the Village to salvation after it was left in shambles years ago. Now holding great imperium. She is poised. Relentless and considerably compassionate on the contrary.

    Powerfully gifted by the Gods. Only those who are chosen leaders are gifted with supernatural abilities. Once they've reached the end of their reign, their superpowers relinquish. Like slivers of dust particles vanished in thin air, as if it were never of existence.

    Now I, nothing like her, next in line. Only I am not yet ready to take my place. Or so I thought. I've daydreamed many times about what powers the Gods would gift me. Until I'm faced with destiny, I cower in my skin like hunt before prey.

It's not as easy as people think it is. I see what The Mother goes through. Most days, she's terribly annoyed. Once in a blue moon, I catch her smiling. Her smiles are never for me though.

Nothing I do seems to please her. I train, she discredits me and says I could have done better. I eat, she takes food out my hand and tells me I've gained too much weight. I wake up late, I'm not productive enough. I go outside, I'm accused of doing bad things. I've gotten used to it though. Her ways and comments don't bother me like they used to when I was young. I feel sorrier for the people who aren't used to her.

She was kind to me at one point. Back when I was about seven. I remember things changing drastically when I turned twelve.

As the full moon settles, the wolves descend.

How daring of Thomas to ride out on his horse to bring back wood for fire. His strong arms and the scent of his warm embrace, lingering on my body even moments after he'd already gone.

While I await his return passing time, by reading poems mother used to write and read to me when I was young. To remember those moments is to cherish those moments.

Settled and snugged sipping tea, covered by the quilt Thomas placed over me moments ago, before I seen shadows casting at the windows. Then again passing by the doors. Fast movements. Could be human, could be animal.

Whatever it is, can obviously sense that I am inside. Perhaps sensing that I am alone. Maybe they waited for this moment. Waited and watched for Thomas to ride off.

I slowly crept to the side of the house to peek out the window. Daggers ready. However, as dark as the night is to be born with sight then blinded in time.

I'm in the middle of nowhere. I will have to use other senses. I can hear swift movements. I can smell the metal of rustic swords.

This is no animal. This is human. The side door creaked shifting my attention. I'm prepared to fight.

Just as I was about to attack whomever came through the door. Thomas appeared and moved about slowly, so as to be sure not to make a noise.

Old panels of the floorboard making it hard as it squeaked with every step he took. Beckoning.

Reluctantly I followed his lead. We escaped through a hatchet he built to blend in with the wooden panels of the floors. A hatchet that led to labyrinths.

Onerous, not being able to be guided by an oil lamp or the flame of a torch. Only that of my hand being led by his through the dark narrow wet crawl spaces.

If not for him, I surely would be lost. Once we've reached outside the labyrinth and had reached a safe distance. Thomas alerted me that upon his leaving he was not alone.

"There were three men at the front and three men at the back of the cottage."

"How did you get away?"

"I snuck in the side door. We must move quickly before they figure out the hatchet. With all things left behind they will have known you were there"

"Me? What makes you so sure they were looking for me?"

"The men wore royal coat of arms. They surely weren't here for me."

"They found me." I said aloud but thought to myself.

"Yes, they've found you and we must move quickly as I'm sure they have summoned all guards by now."

Astonished, we moved through the marsh like hasty mice in the night. Thomas stopped at various precise locations. Collecting bags of supplies at each point. Clearly a well sorted out plan for the means of an escape.

Each contained different materials. The first bag was full of weapons. The second was full of food. The third, he never opened in front of me. Many thoughts were racing through my head. What do we do? Where do we go? Who exactly found me?

ONE
KATIANNA

I can feel the wind with mist in air, I am close to waterfall. I can smell the scent of the sky; I am not grounded.

The birds are flying fast and headed south, which tells me, I am not alone. People are watching. It is so quiet; you could almost hear beating hearts.

The mother has warned me of this day. Warned me that it will come when I least expect it.

"Mountain, near waterfall." I proclaimed. My feet felt like it was sinking into the ground as if I were standing in quicksand.

"Good job Katianna." The father said.

At least I know I have a person. I stood there blindfolded, awaiting the bell, which is signal to run fast and stop just before the edge of the mountains, while channeling my innermost spirit of senses by lighting the Village symbol torch with a flaming arrow that I must gather before edge. Panting becomes me.

Why does it feel like everything I have ever eaten, is suddenly coming up from the pit of my stomach.

Every nerve in my body aroused. I can now hear people gasp; I can hear the whispers.

Thee entire village must be watching. Watching to see if I pass or fail.

They want to know if I am yet ready to take my place as their leader. I'm supposed to be able to connect my mind to the ground, my soul to the sky, and my heart to the spirit of the people, all without sight.

They say if a person cannot make themselves one with the earth, then they certainly cannot make themselves one with their own mind.

If I ran past the ledge, falling fifty feet to the bottom of rubbish, I will have shamed my entire family.

The mother, most of all, who has been training me since I was a young child to take her place. Three failed attempts will deem me unsuited, which will then cause a shift in the success line of leaders.

The bell rings. There is no time for hesitation. So, I run, I run, faster, and faster. Trying to perfectly estimate my speed with distance and time.

Next thing I know, just as I prepared to stop short enough to pick up the bow. I slid off the edge. I knew it when I felt the heat of the flames brush against the tiny hairs on my arms.

One Down.

First-attempt failures are the toughest. Dealing with self-confidence, on top of the callous comments and disappointing those closest to you.

This is the part that's either going to make you or break you. As the day turns into night, I'm sure I am the current gossip of the village.

Have you ever felt like all eyes were on you and that no matter what you do or say, people are only fixated on you? Imagine that time a hundred.

It makes you feel pressured. Pressured to be this perfect mortal because you're basically living your life microscopically.

We gather for dinner feast every evening in the quarter Dutch house, typically when the sun settles.

I cannot help but see The Mothers look of umbrage when our eyes met. After all, what good am I, if not her successor? This burden I must carry on my shoulders, not just my own, but that of an entire Village, is a heavy one.

Other girls are also trained from young to compete, and take my place, if need be.

Blue Village has always chosen a woman as their leader.

Tales circulated about how women holds more power, as they can sway a man's attention, causing distraction.

While other Villages differentiate. Some are led by men.

I've never felt more awkward in my life sitting at the dinner table. As I reach my hand to the basket before me. My hand froze midair.

The Mother clearly using her powers against me. She was gifted as a brainwasher. She can unfreeze, change, and refreeze any object or person to a certain extent.

"That girl mustn't have bread, for she is already too heavy to not know where there is a ledge upon her" the mother said sarcastically.

I've never heard a more stentorian room filled with laughter.

Ha Ha Ha's all over the place.

Mr. Punic was laughing so hard, food was flying out of his big fat mouth. Even the little ones were laughing. Not even knowing what they were laughing at.

As I grew angry rather more than embarrassed, I slammed my hand down to the table, causing all eyes to slowly divert to me.

The room stood still. The air thicker than I remembered it too ever be. My throat constricted. Scratched of dryness.

"Mother." I said staring her down as if no one else in the room existed. "Dare to show me how it's done, last I checked you failed your first two attempts, and barely passed your third."

I could feel the vein in the middle of my forehead pulsating. The palms of my hands were slick with sweat, and my heart was racing ahead of its beats.

In this moment, I do not care of what repercussions I will face. The momentary silence as everyone sunk into their seats, including the father and the siblings, was alluding for sure.

The Mother is to be feared, for she is our leader. She is also the one who taught me to be fearless and to always speak my mind.

As she turned her head slowly toward my direction, I could almost distinctly feel the heat from her eyes as if they were made up of laser beams. If looks could kill, I'd be dead.

"Oh, dear Kati, my child, my only daughter whom I raised, nurtured, and trained. I see you are becoming. So much so that your tongue has forgotten its manners". There was a brief silence before she continued…. "I understand the frustration and failure you must feel, as you know we are all so disappointed. For that reason, only, I am going to give you a pass, just this once." She sipped from her cup of wine graciously.

There was such power behind that subtle response. All I could do was walk away. Walk away with such regret from ever opening my mouth in the first place.

How do you morph extreme humiliation from the inside of a human's soul?

On top of that, the walk from the table to the exit was particularly longer all of a sudden. I thought I'd never make it out of there.

After leaving the dining hall doors. I rested upon the first pillar I stumbled upon. Thinking to myself what now

Barely even having had a moment to catch my breath and fathom what had just occurred. Stacey, whom is like a sister to me, came running up like a puppy greeting its new owner for the first time.

Her strides were off. Her feet looks as if they didn't give the rest of her body a chance to catch up.

It wasn't until now that I noticed she had the most unbalanced, unorganized structure I'd ever seen.

TWO

KATIANNA

"You know she's only being tough on you because she wants you to succeed." Stacey panted heavy while crouching forward resting her hands on her knees. "We all do Kati. Your mother loves you." She continued in between catching breaths.

She pulled loose strands of my hair behind my ear. Her breath slowly returning to its natural state.

"Love me? You're joking, right? If that's what love is, I never want it, ever. She's more imprudent than a vicious animal eating its own young for survival." ……"I truly understand my duties Stacey, I do, but for her to humiliate me in front of everyone like that was wicked. You try having the weight of the world on your shoulders." I tried my best to choke back tears.

"Katianna, look at me, you are strong, smart, and the prettiest girl in Village. You'll get it right next time. Block out the people and pretend as if it's just you out there. And as far as love goes, you do want it. We all do. I watched you since we were little girls finding love in all things. Remember when you use to try on your mother dresses and pretend, we were at your wedding." We both laughed and I suddenly had flashbacks of the times where I wore my mother dresses.

I would make Stacey and Lee act as my witnesses. While I used the life size stuffed animal father gifted me for my ninth birthday, as my husband to be.

"Thanks, I appreciate your kind words." I sighed.

We shared a warm embrace before she added her smart remarks.

"Besides, you were only embarrassed because Lee was there."

She gave me a soft shove before taking off running, knowing that I would give chase.

"Get back here Stace, I'm going to kill you."

"you'll have to catch me first." she replied playfully whilst picking up speed and, running through the halls of the Dutch House.

****

The night was dreary and cold. Alone in my room pacing the floors wondering where I went wrong.

It's hard to concentrate when a million things are pondering in my mind. Suddenly, there's a unique knock at the door.

tap,tap,boom, tap,boom----tap,tap,boom,tap,boom

"Who goes there?" I ask curiously. Waited a few seconds for a response.

There was no answer. Even though I am one of the most protected ladies in the Village. Fear is overpowering protection.

"I said who goes there, answer me immediately, or I will scream for help and whomever you are, you will be locked away." I'd hoped my voice was grim enough.

The door begins too slightly open. Soft and slow. Creepy. As I waited in panic, I grabbed a quill off my desk. Regretting leaving my daggers on the other side of the room.

Not that a quill will, in any way, suffice if the intruder were stronger than the paper it inks on.

"Last warning."

"Oh my, please don't hurt me, Princess."

I recognized the playful voice. It was Lee.

"My goodness Lee, you rather scared me half to death, what are you doing here." My fear was suddenly gone, replaced by butterflies.

He invited himself completely into my chambers, closing the door behind him.

"I came to check on you Princess." he said with such wit.

"Please stop calling me Princess, I am not a Princess." My quarrelsome tongue was enough to receive furrowed eyes.

"My apologies. If not a Princess, then what?"

"A girl. I am just a girl."

Lee helped himself to a seat on the lounge.

"I brought you something." he said looking at me with those dreamy blue eyes of his.

"Really, what'd you bring me? Some dignity?"

"Don't be so hard on yourself. What you did was amazing and took lots of courage. I can't tell you how many girls I've seen back out just before the competition."

"Girls? How many girls do you watch exactly?"

"Not watch. Judge. There is a difference."

He stood up and walked towards me. The shy girl in me walked one step back for each step he took towards me. Until I was cornered and could go no further.

Face-to-face now. Lee was so close I could feel his breathing on my face.

"What's the difference?" I asked. My voice cracked like I'd been dying a thirst all evening.

"You're the difference."

"Really? How so?"

"Well, you're fearless for starters. You're not prissy like the other girls. Not the type of girl afraid to get her hands dirty."

With every word he spoke. The more my body became excited.

"Funny, maybe you should tell that to The Mother."

"It doesn't matter what she sees or what anyone else knows or thinks. It's about who you are when no one's watching."

As he got even closer, he leaned in. I wanted him so badly to kiss me at this moment.

I know he knows it. He can see it in my eyes. Glaring. He can feel it off my body signals.

As I waited for him, lusting. He, instead of a kiss, pulled out a piece of bread.

"Enjoy it." he said while walking away towards the door. He looked back at me before completely leaving and said "Princess." I gazed to him "You will never be just a girl."

The bad girl in me wanted to pull him back and indulge. However, I do not know if he feels the same way for me as I do for him, and I've already made a fool of myself once. I certainly will not do it again.

My attraction for Lee grew stronger over the years. He certainly is not the little snaggle tooth boy I remembered him to be.

He now stands over 6 feet tall, with the body of a masculine God.

The curves of his chest cut as if all he does is spend his days training, his jaw tight, and his sea blue eyes that I find myself getting lost in every time he's around.

His nose, perfectly symmetrical on his face. The clean hairless face that sometimes grows signs of stubble when he goes without shaving, and his blonde pendulous hair that lays flat when he's been sweating.

The skin on his arms inked with symbolic definitions. He's certainly a man now.

****

That night, I barely slept. I tossed and turned all night. Thinking about the fall, about Lee (as I always have since we were nine), and about how I am to face The Mother tomorrow.

Princess, you will never be just a girl.

THREE

KATIANNA

The next morning. I awoke, only to find The Mother sitting already at my bedside. As she does, whenever we are at differences.

"So beautiful, even upon waking up. Whereas the rest of us must freshen up to look as pretty, as you, and you wonder why the others are covetous." Her eyes narrowed looking far off in the distance towards the window.

As if she could see the outside from where she sat. Only the stone walls were as there as they were burly. She saw nothing.

I sat up. Ready for whatever was coming my way. For, I knew it was becoming.

"Mother, I'm sorry for what happened at dinner."
She cut me off.

"Shhh my child. All is forgiven and forgotten. Katianna, I know I trained you to perfection. I also know you will not let our hard work, blood, sweat, tears, and sleepless nights, go to waste….It is only a matter of time. You'll know when you're ready. For it will be when the world is ready to receive you."

We both sat in silence. I couldn't figure out if this was a good thing or a bad thing.

"Never let words overpower your mind enough to create a reaction. Not even from me. People are going to say things about you all the time, and if every time they do, you simply lose it. Well then, you've lost."

She so calmly spoke while retrieving the hairbrush from my bedside and started brushing my hair like she did when I was a little girl.

"I can't believe you still have this brush. I gave this to you so long ago. It's a family air loom you know. A relic given to me by my mother, from her mother, from her mother, and now to you, and hopefully one day you'll give it to your daughter. The stones alone on this brush is worth more than this Village."

"Yes Mother, I know. That is why I have taken such good care of it. No other brush brushes my hair like it. It's my favorite."

"Come now." The Mother said while pulling me up from bed.

"Get ready and meet me in the green room. I have a surprise for you."

Excited to see what this surprise was. I scurried to and out of the bath and headed to the green room.

The green room is a sanctuary place for The Mother. She goes there to have tea, to read, and ultimately, to think and relax.

No one is allowed in the green room. Only her maiden, when she needs something brought to her. I can count on one hand how many times I've seen the inside of that room. All those times I was just a child wandering about playing hide and seek with Lee and Stacey.

Each time I got caught, I was scolded. Something is up, that she invited me there.

The doors were ajar upon my arrival. The Mother was sitting, already sipping tea. I knocked.

"Please come in Kati."

Upon opening the doors, thinking how different this room looked now, than from when I was younger.

Big windows that viewed the mountains. Fresh flowers everywhere. Stunning. I sat at the table across from The Mother.

I couldn't help but notice the big black box with a red bow sitting in the corner.

"The box is for you. I want you to open it."

The box was detailed. Engraved with my name on it. I pulled the bow tie exposing its content, and there lies a beautiful black gown.

I lifted it out of its house and inspected it in awe. It was a sparkly one-sleeved, off-the-shoulder, belted, mermaid hem formal dress with a skirt made of silk and added velvet trims. The most expensive dress I had ever seen.

"Mother it's gorgeous. Thank you so much" I couldn't take my eyes off it.

"I'm glad you like it, because I want you to wear it next week."

"Next week, for what?"

"For the Blackfield Festival, of course."

"You didn't forget again, did you?" She said looking at me like she'll literally kill me.

"Of course, not" I lied with such ease.

"Good, because everyone will be there and there are very powerful and rich men shipping in, as well as other leaders.

Who knows, maybe you will find a lucky man. Handsome. Someone of great stature. An astounding suitor."

"Mother, I do not want a man."

"Child, please. Everyone wants a man. From the moment we come of age." She smiled an almost smile before adding. "Don't forget to make your mask wonderful. There is a prize."

The BlackField is a huge gathering Blue Village hosts every year consisting of an all-black dinner attire, handmade masquerades, elegant dancing, fine foods and wines, games and prizes, and most importantly a hand in marriage.

Every year an eligible bachelor of the highest multitude comes to the Village, scopes out all the ladies, and at the end of the night, purposes marriage to one lucky lady, in front of everyone.

Shall she choose to accept, a ceremony is held at that very same moment. The girls in the Village are quite excited. Especially Stacey.

Last year Lady Kennedy was chosen. I am never excited about it because I believe in falling in love the right way. Not being picked and hauled off by someone I don't know just because he has wealth.

Besides, no one will ever pick me because I am the daughter of a Village leader.

"You may go." The Mother said as she continued to sip tea.

I ran over and gave her a big hug. Even though she is not one for affection. Of course, she shooed me away.

****

Days leading up to the *Black Field festival* were spent training.

The Mother made me such a tight and disciplined schedule.

I mostly trained on the bow and arrow with David. I had to sneak in times to spend with Stacey.

I trained day and night.

Exhaustion becomes me. I never thought I'd be looking forward to the festival. As it meant having a day off from training for me.

There were gowns, brushes, jewelry and giddy girls everywhere. All hoping to be the lucky girl, I suppose.

Wishing I could be a part of it led to nothing but hopeless hope.

There was always something about getting ready, doing hair and makeup with the others. Or at least Stacey, that made me feel an ounce of being a girl.

Being that I am the daughter of the Village leader, my entrance to the dinner portion of the festival will be separate. At least for now, I can partake in the regular day activities.

Ships were rolling in. Bountiful men and leaders were arriving. Everyone looked so clean and serious.

Only the top tier of each leader's village was invited.

The goal for all is to bring back trades of any sort that will enrich their village furthermore, also to form strong alliances.

Blue Village always held the upper hand. We are the main source of crops. We normally trade with black for their fine furs and woods.

There I stood in the window, watching people arrive with luggage, seeing The Mother greet them with such hospitality.

"Don't worry Kati, I'm sure there's a knight and shining armor for you."

Stacey burst into my chambers and hopped on my bed.

"So, what are you wearing tonight?" She asked me.
"Nothing special, just a gown."

"Right." She responded eyeing me with suspension.

"Well come now, let's get out there and make our rounds. The games are beginning, and I want good seats for the Jousting."

Jousting was the biggest event next to the proposal.

When a Knight wins at Jousting, he then rides his horse around the crowd until he finds a lady with whom he's fond, and just before he presents her with a rose and a ticket for a private dinner invitation, he unmasks himself, exposing his identity in hopes to win the heart of his interest. It is all the rave.

Apparently, everyone here knows who I am. People were stopping me to say hello. Some elders held my hand telling me how big I'd gotten.

Others, the youngers, were shooting me looks of thy enemy.

Furthermore, running around with Stacey kept my mind off so many things.

We painted the faces of the children. My own younger brothers included. We played archery. Which I won twice.

Stumbling about was Lady Willow, accompanied by her two minions Mia and Mya, twins from the White Village next over.

Willow and I have always been in comparisons. She too is next in line as a Village leader.

"I see the vertical finally caught up with the horizontal." Willow said sarcastically as her two minions snickered.

Stacey whispered to me that it wasn't worth it and tried to pull me along. Knowing I should listen to her, as well as what mother just told me about not letting words get to me. However, I am not there yet.

"Lady Willow. I see the weight won't stop putting on, is that a girdle? You poor thing. Must be difficult to breathe in that thing while you stuff your face."

She lowered the piece of cake she had already taken bites of. Even her ladies were speechless. They stormed off mumbling.

"Katianna you bad bad girl." Stacey said as we both walked away laughing. The adrenaline rush I felt after winning round one against Willow, was the sweetest nectar my lips ever longed for.

There was an announcement on the dome speakers as we were just about to play a game of finding the sacred rock with the hidden treasure inside.

"The Jousting will begin in fifteen minutes."

FOUR
KATIANNA

Everyone rushed past nearly knocking each other down to get good seats in the stadium. Stacey dragged me about, as I was not moving fast enough for her.

"Great, just great." she muttered.

"Calm down, we can still see clearly."

"Easy for you to say. This is by choice for you. You could be up there with your mom and dad."

"I know that, but I don't want to be in the spotlight. I am fine, right here with you."

The Jousting began and the stadium is so loud I could barely hear whatever it is Stacey was saying. There were to be four rounds and then a championship round. Eight different colors representing the eight Villages.

Our color is blue. The winner from each round will advance until he reaches the championship. The most thrilling part is not knowing who's underneath those helmets.

I'm not even sure who will be representing blue this year. The first-round winner was black who won against yellow, then green wins against white, blue wins over purple, and red wins against brown.

The next round is between blue and red. This one was exciting for our village because if blue lose, were out. Our Village consists of very vigorous and competitive men.

As the horses were released from the pits. Lances were drawn as they charged toward each other. The stadium held its breath. No one wins. Neither man was knocked down. So, they go again. This time with more aggression. Blue wins.

"We win, we won." Stacey said jumping up and down and screaming from the top of her lungs as did everyone else, including me. We were all so proud to be blue.

I looked across the way and saw my parents hugging and smiling. What a joyous moment. I long for that smile of hers. For her to be as proud of me one day as she is in this very moment.

Black and green is now up, and whichever winner will face blue in the championship. Black wins. The excitement coming from that Village was just as hyper as do us.

The announcer came on once more.

"Ladies and gentlemen, this is the moment we've all been waiting for. Who will take the title this year claiming victory for their Village and claiming the heart of one lucky lady. Will it be black?" The crowd cheered.

"Will it be blue?" The crowd cheered even louder.

"May the best knight win."

The horses came flying out and the knights were focused and ready. As we all stood by holding our breath.

Much to our despise, black wins, knocking blue down terribly. So much so, that blue is believed to be injured.

It was supposed to be a friendly competition, not meant to harm anyone.

As the crowd booed and blue was carried away to seek medical attention in the infirmary. The black Knight retrieved the gold rose and the sealed stamped envelope to set forth his search.

He rounded about at least three times over by now. Must be looking for a specific lady in the crowd. Suddenly as his horse went by, I couldn't help but feel he locked eyes with me although he was wearing a helmet.

"Oh my god, Katianna, he looked at you.'"

"He did not."

"Did too."

"He did not."

She grabbed me by the shoulders.

"HE DID TOO." Stacey was yelling at this point.

As the horse came about the fourth time, he suddenly stopped. He jumped down from his horse and over the banister. My eyes were fixated on him, as it seemed his were on mine. He stopped right before me and took off his helmet.

"For you, my lady." My heart engrossed in my chest. His sweaty hair stuck to his forehead. His eyes searched mines for a sliver of admiration.

He pleaded with me to take his golden rose. Everyone staring. Waiting for my response. My goodness he is so handsome. I've never seen him before.

I purposely retreated my blush. Not wanting to appear enthralled.

"Thank you." I said as I took the golden rose. In complete shock. Everyone lingered around in awe.

He took my hand and planted a kiss. His full lips were softer to my skin, than they appeared to be to my sight.

"Save me the last dance?"

"Maybe." I replied. The blush on my face making a debut against my will.

With all the flirting and excitement going on. I looked down at the tents where the infirmary was set up, and I could see Lee.

Lee was blue, and he was looking directly at me taking the rose. Once our eyes met, he walked off the fields and into the woods riding his horse.

I felt terrible but confused. Was he jealous? If he had won, would he have given me the rose? So many questions were in my mind. More importantly, was he ok from injury?

I must go after him. As I know he most certainly would go after me. I ran down the steps ignoring everyone's calls, asking me what happened and where I was going. Into the woods, where all ladies are taught, never to enter alone.

There is an old tale about a monster living in the woods who takes ladies and slit their wrist for the thirst of blood and sacrifices them to cleanse their souls.

At this moment, I am not thinking, nor am I afraid. I just want to find him. Not too long after I entered the red woods, did I find Lee skipping rocks by the riverbank.

"Lee." I called to him softly while resting my hand on his shoulder. He would not turn around to face me.

"Please talk to me, I saw you running into the woods after." He cut me off.

"You shouldn't be here. Your mother will kill us both. Go back to your boyfriend."

"He is not my boyfriend."

"So why would you take a gold rose from him? We all know what that represents."

"It means nothing."

"Really? Then why were you smiling ear to ear?" It was at that moment that I realized my attempt to hold back my blush, in fact, failed. I hadn't been aware that I even smiled that hard. A little maybe, but not that hard.

An awkward moment of silence stood frozen. Worse than ice on the bed of a lake.

"Why do you care?"

"I don't."

"Really. Well then why are we talking about him instead of you telling me why you ran into the woods?"

"I just came here to clear my head, if that's alright with you."

"Well then, I shall just join you." I sat down cross legged on the floor next to him.

"My god, you are the most exasperating person I know."

"I'll take that as a compliment." "How come you never told me you were entering the Jousting competition?" He joined me on the floor.

"Because I wanted to spare myself of the exact humiliation that I am feeling right now."

I grabbed his hand.

"You know, I, of all people, know exactly what that feels like, but did you hear that crowd go wild when you won against red? That is what the people will remember."

"No, they will remember, blue, the one who didn't win, and they will remember how black took the show and gave you the gold rose, not me." I took my hand to guide his chin up and face towards me.

"A wise man once told me it doesn't matter what anyone thinks, it only matters what you do when no one's watching." I paused, then continued. "Forget about black, forget about the stupid rose. I am not sitting at his side after running behind him through the woods. I am next to you, aren't I?"

Lee looked over at me. It was a different look. One I've never noticed before, and I was sure I knew of all his looks.

Our eyes locked, the chemistry is there. I know he feels it too. He moved his hands closer to mine. I could bear my feelings no longer.

I wanted to taste his lips. So, I kissed him. Passionately. He did not protest. Instead, he pulled me in closer to him. Deep lingering while he held the back of my neck.

The gesture was perceived and reciprocated. The kiss became vehement. As I am now lost in him. I sat on top of him, as he held my back while my tongue glided around the sweet taste of his. Never wanting this moment to end.

However, he wanted to settle down before we took it too far. I didn't want him to stop so I kissed the palm of his hand using tongue giving a pleasurable bite.

"Touch me." I whispered softly in his ear.

He began to kiss my shoulders and my neck while gripping my breast. My body is doing things I've never felt before.

My lady part moistened with slickness. Throbbing between my thighs. We began undressing each other's tops. I gasped hard when his warm mouth touched my skin. Trailing his tongue on my collar bone.

A rush of sensation as he started sucking on my breast causing my nipples to erect. Then making his way back up sucking on my neck making me even more aroused.

Neither of us cared about what's around us. Then, he suddenly slowed down.

"What's wrong?" I asked.

"Princess, I don't want to take advantage. If I have you, there is no coming back from that."

I brung his face up to mine and looked him in his eyes.

"Do you want me?" "Tell me you don't want me, and I'll leave right now."

He leaned in, whispered in my ear. "I want you more than you could ever imagine."

"Then I am telling you, you can have me." ……
"Touch me." My eyes pleaded his for his mercy.

He grabbed me eagerly and kissed me again. His hands caressing my cunt. Awakening a vibration of dopamine in my brain.

He planted kisses on my neck and took my breast in his mouth once more while I sucked in a sharp breath and let off soft moans.

With each stroke of his hand against the curves of my back, made me grind on him harder. Yearning for his deep touch.

"Princess." he whispers.

I turned into him. "You're not going to take me, are you?" I knew it, the way he slowed down.

He bit into my shoulder softly.

"Believe me I want you, since we were nine. Since the day I brought you your first dandelion, and I'd hope you were wishing to one day be with me when you blew at it. I know how much your virtue means to you, and although you make it hard, I can control myself long enough to wait for you when the time is right. When you are mines, and I, yours."

I dropped my head onto his shoulder.

"Look at me." he demanded while lifting my head to stare him in his eyes.

"The time will come, and when it does, I will make countless love to you, until the Villagers can't take hearing you scream from the pleasures of my tongue and makes complaints about us."

I sighed….. "You really should choose your words carefully then if you want us to wait."

I caressed the girth of his shaft while sending my tongue in circles around his ear and neck. Feeling him grow from the touch of my hands.

Even though we're waiting, doesn't mean I won't tease. At least I now know he did share the same feelings as I. Since we were nine.

We could not stay off each other. One kiss, and boom. After a while, we both knew we had to head back before The Mother sent a search team out for me. Plus, we had to get ready for the black dinner.

"I will walk back, so there is no gossip."

"You will do no such thing. I'm going to ride you on my horse."

He picked me up and lifted me onto the horse and sat me in front of him while we rode back into Village.

That ride was great. Peaceful. Having his arms enveloped around me while having his body so close to mine.

Amazing how a kiss and touch changes the dynamic of a friendship to more than. I did not want to go back to reality after the undying new world I discovered.

I had my eyes closed almost the entire ride back. I have this weird thing with me where I close my eyes to feel more connected. I brush my teeth, I close my eyes, I bathe, I close my eyes, I eat, I close my eyes. It makes me feel more in tune with whatever I'm doing.

Some sort of deep connection to my mind. Upon arriving, the festivities were still taking place. I was hoping to rush to my room without being noticed.

"Katianna." A deep stern voice alarmed me. It was The Father.

"Where have you been daughter? Your mother has been looking for you everywhere. She said something about someone seeing you run off into the woods."

"Don't be silly father." I walked to greet him.
"I got lost in playing some of the games."

He looked at me, second guessing the answer I had given.

"Well then get ready for dinner, and you will be sitting with us. Not off to the side with other ladies. You are a part of this family."

"Yes Father."

I scurried away before he could notice the tearing in my clothes.

FIVE
KATIANNA

Inside my room now, I laid on my bed with pondering thoughts. I cannot believe what just happened between Lee and me.

I wonder how he's feeling. What he's thinking. My heart feels full. All I could do was smile.

The bath I took was extra relaxing today. After getting ready, I waited for the Dutchmen to escort me down.

The Mother and The Father were to go first. Then the siblings, then me last. Because this is mother's court, we must be introduced. The last thing I wanted was all eyes on me, again.

The Dutchmen arrived and escorted us all to the stairs, where everyone waited down at the bottom to greet.

"I bestow unto you. Deities Mary-Ann and Joe."

Everyone clapped.

"I bestow unto you. The royal children Joe jr. and Noah."

My little brothers, as cute as they are, a handful. Noah was running the other way up the stairs while they were being announced. Everyone admired them and had a good laugh.

"I bestow unto you the beautiful Lady Katianna."

As I walked down the steps I could hear a lot of people in awe, a lot of people saying how stunning I looked. Lee is gazing into my eyes. The black knight with the golden rose is also gazing into my eyes.

Thank God that entrance is over. I thought to myself.

"We welcome you all into our homes and hope that you all find comfort and happiness here." The mother proclaimed as she raised her glass. "Happy Trading."
"Hear hear." the room responded.

At dinner, I must sit with my family at the head of the table allowing us to have a view of everyone. Lee is sitting next to Lady Hallie.

I can't help but notice the two being chummy. Dinner was annoying, as I had to sit there for what felt like hours enduring boring stories from the guests that sat next to us and watching Lee flirt right in front of my face after we sealed our fate to one another.

Or at least that's what I deemed it to be after all the kissing and touching we were doing. Once dinner was over, we all get to mingle and dance, and I could finally socialize. The first person I went for was Lee of course.
"Katianna, look at you, you are gorgeous."
"Thanks Stacey, so are you."

"Come, let's dance." She pulled me to the dance floor. All the while, I was looking for Lees face in the crowd of hundreds of people.

Eventually, I gave up, and joined in on the fun. We danced so hard for what seemed to be an eternity.

The pain in my heels reflecting. Remembering what it is and is not meant for. I forgot where I was for a moment.

Next thing I know the music slowed down. This part is for lovers I thought to myself. Think I'll sit this one out.

The Mother and The Father shared the first slow dance. Other couples followed. It was so sweet.

One of the men from the other Village came and asked Stacey for her hand to dance. She was excited. I was happy for her. It was joyous watching all the couples. I love, love.

Out of nowhere, a hand extended out to me asking to dance. It was him. The Black Knight.

"May I have this dance."

"You may." I felt regret taking his hand to dance, but why should I, when Lee is probably somewhere making out with that skank from dinner.

So I went, and I danced slowly with the Black knight.

"Your beautiful." he whispered to me.

"Right, I bet you tell that to all the girls."
"Not necessarily. ".. "Are you always this tough, or you're just giving me a hard time."
"Sorry, no."

"It's ok, you seem a little tense. Let me help lighten your mood."

He said as he spun me around and then spun me into him so that he was holding me from behind. He handled me so well.

He was smooth. Before I knew it, it was just us on the dance floor with everyone watching. I must admit, he had such elegant moves, you wouldn't have been able to tell that I didn't know the dance. It was a touching moment.

When he dipped me, I saw Lee. Standing there, watching. Now why is he always popping out of nowhere and where was he when I was looking for him?

When the dance ended, everyone clapped, and others joined back on the dance floor. Lee even found a partner and danced with her.

Sparking an outrage inside of me I could not control. I couldn't stand to see it. I grabbed him out of the crowd. "Outside. NOW." I demanded.

We walked out the doors and into the dead cold night.

"What the hell was that?" I asked.

"I should be asking you the same."

"So, what is this, tit for tat now."

"Katianna are you serious. You're jealous of some girl I don't even know or care about. Meanwhile I had to watch you. Not once, but twice, with the same guy trying to woo you over and you fall for it."

"Nobody is wooing me. You were nowhere to be found."

"So, I'm nowhere to be found, green light on the next guy then."

"Lee, it's not like that."

"What's it like then. Tell me…..Tell me so that I would know what to do. That girl means nothing to me, but you can't expect to do whatever you want and expect me to sit around like a puppy, begging you to pick me."

"You're not a puppy Lee and I don't expect anything from you."

Thought it might be best if I walked away.

"Right, leave, walk away, because that's going to solve this issue."

I turned back around to him.

"You know what Lee. I have all eyes on me constantly. I am just playing the part to be nice because I am the people's future leader, what's your excuse."

"Don't you give me that bullshit. Just because you're prominent doesn't mean you get to flaunt around with other guys. Letting them learn you and touch you. Do you like that guy? Tell me now."

"Of course, not."

"Then why would you take his rose and invitation, then turn around and dance the night away with him."

I couldn't help but let the tears form in my eyes. The last thing I wanted was to hurt Lee.

He couldn't stand to see me sad. He brought me into him, holding me and wiping my tears away.

"Katianna, I'm sorry my princess." He said while kissing my forehead.

"I didn't mean to make you cry. I can't stand to see it. Please stop. Nothing ever happened between me and that girl. Or me and any other girl. My heart is with you. I promise. I know you have a duty to uphold, and I'm being jealous. I can't help it. Do you know how sexy you are? If a man is not the least bit jealous, then he's not the one for you." A small smile cracked upon my lips.

"Now there's my girl."

"Lee, I want you and only you. I'm sorry that these things make you uncomfortable. It was only until today I even knew we were………. whatever we are, I know it happened fast and we didn't even talk about it, but if I'm being honest, I've been having feelings for you for the longest time now."

"It's so weird because so did I. Isn't it amazing how two people could have the same feeling for so long. I'm going to be honest, seeing you jealous over me was so sexy."

"Shut up." I said pushing him.

"Let's go back inside, it's getting cold out here."

We walked back inside and immediately Stacey grabbed me.

"Well, hello, my best friend who I rarely get to see now. Is there something going on that I should know about?"

"Something like what?"

I began to walk fast as in to avoid her questions.

"You know dam well what. With you and Lee. First you run off behind him, now you two come back from outside together. Do tell?"

"There is nothing to tell." I couldn't help but blush.

"Liar. You're keeping secrets. Tell me tell me tell me." Stacey insisted and thinking she would get it out of me by tickling me half to death.

The Mother gathered the crowd about to make an announcement.

"The time has come for the main event. The special hand in marriage ceremony. Best be of luck to all the ladies."

Ladies all over crossed their fingers in hopes they were chosen, and perhaps would suddenly gain a better life. The man in question will step forward and proclaim a hand in marriage.

I sipped my wine and sat back to enjoy the charades. The room was cheerful as everyone looked to their left and to their right. To see which man was coming forward. Suddenly, The Black Knight was at my feet. Down on one knee with the most beautiful ring I've ever seen.

"Katianna, will you be my forever lady, will you marry me? I know we don't know each other, but given the chance that will change, I will protect you and make you happy."

I spit my sip of wine back into the glass.

"Quit playing and get up from there." I whispered to him. Prudently watchful. As discreet as I can be.

"I assure you this is not a joke. I have already asked your parents for your hand. They've given their blessing."

I looked over to see the mother and the father with their signal of approval. I looked at Lee who was giving me.

I dare you eyes.

I looked all around at all the many faces. My heart pounding trying to escape its chambers. How could this be happening.

"I don't know what to say." I replied.

"Say yes. Please….. say yes." He pleaded.

"I don't even know your name, please get up."

Someone yelled.

"Say yes already, we don't got all day."

Reluctant to answer. As I look over at The Mother. If I said yes, she'd finally be proud of me but as I look to Lee my heart just won't let me accept this proposal. Not just because of him, but because it doesn't feel right.

"I can't I'm sorry."

I ran out of the room so fast. Something that's seemingly becoming of me. This is not how it's supposed to be.

Running out of the room I hear other ladies screaming, and in this moment, I just want to escape this place forever. Never looking back or having to justify my every waking movement.

"I'll marry you." "She failed her challenge anyways."

The voices of many ladies. In this moment, I wished to be invisible and alone, so I kept running.

No direction, nothing on my back but a weighted gown. Not even a weapon, nothing merely enough to protect myself from harm, or the cold, or hunger, or the never-before-seen heretics.

I ran until my body gave out. Maybe I'll start over. A new form of life, with animals instead of humans. They cannot pressure me or break my heart.

Here I go again. Reacting before, I think. Always fight or flight, ask questions later. If there were even a sliver of truth to there being a monster in the redwoods, I certainly just ran into the lion's den.

Immediately regretting my decision. However, not enough to turn me around.

SIX
LEE

Morning risen, and there was still no sign of return. Every single man was sent to cover grounds all night long.

With no luck, the people are frantic. Already in talks about who will take place as a leader if Katianna doesn't come back.

I've always hated that. How people treat people like their easily disposable. Always in a rush to replace one with another.

As if one's life was merely a replica of an actual human borrowing a body for the sake of a soul. Katianna is irreplaceable.

"This is all your fault." Mary-Ann angrily accused me.

"Madam, I apologize that you feel that way, but I will not apologize for the way that I feel about your daughter."

"The way you feel about my daughter. Ha. That's a joke. What way could you possibly feel about my daughter, you don't even know my daughter."

"My only concern is to find her safe and sound."

"You will do no such thing. I don't want you anywhere near my daughter. As a matter of fact, if I find that you come anywhere near her ever again, I will order you to be exiled."

I bowed before her.

"With all due respect, that is a promise that I cannot keep. Your daughter is amazing, and I will never stop fighting for her."

"Boy, please. You're not even man enough to bring her the golden rose, how could a simple boy like you ever protect her. She is Prominent to this Village, next in line. She should be focused and marrying a man of great stature. You're a distraction. Always have been. What she sees in you, I haven't a clue. You're a commoner."

I walked away from the controversy before things got out of control. No words of hers will ever resonate. I know she speaks from hurt.

Even if she tries her best to hide it. Even though she treats her daughter like she's nothing more than an object. I know better.

Her harsh ways are a defense mechanism. She loves her daughter more than she lets on.

My love now professed. In front of hundreds. Now all the Villages in attendance to the Blackfield Festival are aware, not just ours alone. I don't care at all. Not even a little.

Before leaving completely I shared more words "Maybe instead of scolding me, you should be asking yourself why your daughter wanted so desperately to get away. I assure you; it was not to get away from me."

I walked away graciously. Even though my adrenaline pumped a spruce of ego.

I'm not even sure why Mary-Ann treated me this way now. Maybe she looked at me differently since I became of age. Maybe she knew I favored her daughter.

She's always treated me like a child of her own my whole childhood. Sometimes more than my own parents.

She'd always let me and Stacey play with Katianna in the fields outside the Village. She'd always invite me to stay for supper.

Even once, she held a birthday party for me in the Dutch house. Had the baker, bake me the biggest cake I had ever seen. It towered taller than me. At that time. My eleventh birthday. I will never forget blowing out the candles, and what I'd wish for.

I guess times have changed. She's changed. Or maybe that was always who she was, and I just didn't notice because I was a child with not a clue in the world. Whatever the case, her like for me had gone away many moons ago.

BAYE ÇILLAGE
(BLUE VILLAGE)

Joe, I want that boy beheaded." Mary-Ann angrily expressed.

"Beheaded? Mary-Ann, you can do no such thing. Love is not treason."

"Love? Joe please don't tell me you agree, do not go against me, she is your daughter to."

"My dear, I am not going against you. Right now, we have the least bit of answers, let us await her return. The truth will prevail."

Mary-Ann leaned against the window, looking down watching the men gather gear and scramble about. The father walked over to her, hugging her from behind. An attempt to comfort.

"Remember how much you hated me when we first met. When we were forced to marry, you nearly grew sick to your stomach. You were opposed to our union."

"Yes, but that was different."

"No difference, you too, wanted to follow your heart. The rules back then were rather more complicated. We learned to get along and eventually fell in love. You cannot have the boy killed just because he professed his love for her. If things worked like that, you would take many heads. As there are plenty of people who loves our daughter. She's admired by every man in court. Our daughter has blossomed like the beautiful roses in your garden."

He turned her around so that they were face to face. The only person in the world that she folds to. He took his hand to softly lift her chin up, to look her in the eyes.

"Let's not control her so much that we push her away, give her time."

"Time is the one thing we don't have."

Mary-Ann walked away, but before she walked out completely.

"That boy suddenly loves our daughter?"

"A boy that would dare challenge you, is indeed, a fool in love."

Two days have passed. Mary-Ann and the Village grew frightened by the day, minute, second. There were plenty of speculations.

"Maybe she got caught by the monster in the woods." Lady Lucette said.

"Or maybe she started a new life in a different Village." Lady Iris said.

People gathered around the evening after Kati's disappearance, lighting lanterns. Letting them sail off into the sky. Praying for her safe return. Lantern lightings, the most sacred of rituals to Blue. Done to call upon the spirit for guidance. To return lost souls back to the Village.

Ladies doubled up on training. As their parents predicted they could possibly be the next leader. Suddenly everyone's a warrioress.

"Lee, we must do something. My best friend is out there. Alone, scared, tired, hungry, cold and defenseless. God knows what else." Stacey worried.

"She is smart and resourceful. Trust me if she wanted to come home. She'd be here by now. She trailed these woods and mountains better than anybody I know. She's not lost, just confused."

"Well, you're her bloody boy toy for God sakes, do something about it. Or should I go ask the black knight." Lee looked over at Stacey like he wishes he could hit a girl.

"I'm sorry Lee, I didn't mean it like that. Although you should know, he's still here. Every Village has left back home, and he's stayed back. Why do you think that is?"

"I do not care of his presence; he is not a worry for me. I will find her, and it is not a rescue mission, she's far more capable than you know, my only hope is to plead with her to come back."

"Can I come? Please?"

"No, this is no task for a lady. Besides we both know she'll kill me herself if I let anything happen to you."

Stacey sighed in annoyance and crossed her arms. In the way that children cross their arms when they don't get their way. Pouty lips and furrowed eyebrows.

Walking past the Great Hall. Mary-Ann surprisingly called out to Lee.

"Boy." she yelled.

Sitting on the throne next to Joe. Seven guards standing right beside the leader. The Black Knight (TBN) included. Lee bowed before her.

"How could I possibly be of service to you, Village Leader?" Lee asked sarcastically.

"Charming. My husband and I have declared that you will be a part of tonight's search hunt for our daughter. To be departed just before dusk."

"Why me? I thought I was hated?"

"Make no mistake boy, you are very much displeasing and disrespectful to my court. However, my husband believes you could be of service. Therefore, you will go."

She continued. "You will be joining The Black Knight, as he will head this search."

"I beg your pardon." Lee proclaimed.

"You will do as I say, or you will be vanished."
The Black Knight stood there with a smirk on his face, before stepping forward.

"I have a plan, you will follow my lead, I will get you caught up with the plan before we set out."

"I'm sorry, follow who, and do what? Who made you the Monarch?"

"Why don't we step outside, and I'll show you."

The Black Knight attempted to walk down the steps, but Mary-Ann extended her reach by freezing him with her powers.

"Enough." She yelled "Save the vigorous ploys for when she returns. For now, I'm counting on both of you to bring my daughter home. Safely."

Mary-Ann whispered to David.

"Follow behind at a distance, and make sure they don't kill each other."

David is a childhood friend of the mother. She keeps him as her advisor. A man of different religious beliefs. Some call him a prophet. Others say he's pagan.

They believe he can heal the sick with gifted hands and natural remedies. They also believe he can see into the future. Many Villagers believe he practices witchcraft.

None of that matter though, as long as he stands by Mary-Ann's side. He is protected and untouchable. David is also extremely skillful with the bow and arrow. Once seen shooting a bird out of the sky. The say he's the more proficient one of all.

The woman who is now his wife was once said to be sick from a plague that occurred thirteen years ago in a nearby Village. She never comes out. He brings food back to their chambers.

One of the guards once claimed to have seen her face when he caught a glimpse inside their chambers before the door shut. He said she only had half a face.

****

The meeting began for tonight's search. The Black Knight announced they would be taking boats to begin searching other Villages and all the grounds and woods nearby. He was to have a crew to stay on board the ship and the rest to set out on foot. There were to be one boat per Village.

"I will send signals of glaring lights pointed at the skies just north of the borders. That will be que to storm the Villages at the same time. We will meet in the middle of the waters if there's any trouble. Mary advises us to use excessive force only if we must."

"I urge you all to bring warm clothes. The food will be supplied at each Village we stop, upon Mary's order. Men, kiss your wives and children and let us all pray for a safe return. Most importantly let us find Katianna, my future wife."

The men all stomped and cheered. A room full of savages. All except Lee. Hearing another man claim Katianna as his own, was vulgar, to say the least.

However, Lee had a plan of his own. Therefore, keeping his composure would be the wisest decision. He made sure to fall into the background.

Apart of his plan is to go unnoticed. To break away from the group and go off on his own. If anyone would be successful at finding and bringing Katianna home, it would be Lee himself.

Moments away from the voyage Lee was presented with a rather unusual opportunity while preparing in his room.

"I dare not to be deceived or disappointed. I've been told by David that you have my daughter's purest intentions in your heart."

A confused Lee

"He told you what."

"Told me that you're an honorable man. That you're the son of Lieth and Lady Maribelle. Two very trustworthy people."

"And."

"And I want you to captain the ship."

Me?"

"Yes, you."

"And what of the word of your wife."

"Let me deal with my wife. You just take this opportunity to prove yourself."

As Lee sat there wrapping up rope and gathering bows.

"I do not pry my self-worth on scoundrel and acceptance. The mere idea of me captaining the ship to prove anything is beneath me and everything I stand for."

As Joe sighed

"I won't scrunt, this is for her, not me, not her mother, not even you. I know you'll make a wise decision."

"Suppose I even entertained that thought. With Mary so close at The Black Knights' graces, how would she relinquish any duty given to him and pass to me."

"There's more than one ship, no one said you'll be on the same crew. I can make arrangements."

"And what makes you think I can do so, or that I even have the experience."

"You think I would present this opportunity to you if I haven't already done my homework? Your good, and she needs you."

Joe walked away. Perhaps in the back of his mind he hoped Lee would do the honorable thing.

In that moment Lee knew he'd do anything asked of him if it meant saving her.

The men began gathering at the front gates. Saying farewells to their families. Setting out on this hunt could take days, even weeks.

In all hopes of executing a perfect plan, one must always be prepared for failure. Failure meant some may not make it back home.

Mary's Village is a very popular yet an envious one. One with many Allies turned enemies and not to mention the traitors lurking within the walls.

Families waited around the docks. Crying wives and children. Praying priest, all things of the sort.

All my captains front and center." the black knight yelled.

As Lee stepped forward, the Black Knight jumped down from the docks landing.

"I don't think you heard me, I said captains, not helpers."

Lee stood straight faced and unbothered.

Have no one told you, I was requested at the hands of your grace."

Joe invertedly gave the nod. Thus, leaving the Black Knight no other choice.

He was sure to leave Lee the less equipped boat with the less prepared fighters. Of course, this was a desperate plea to show him up, but to no avail will that stand in the way.

****

Into the frigid night. The boats set sail. One could barely even see their own hand before them.

Much to Lees advantage he knew the waters and woods like the back of his hand. He and his sister Allison roamed them and traveled them for many years in their childhood.

It was the one place Mary-Ann didn't let Katianna go. It wasn't long on the waters before the men spotted an unusual figure by the village nearby.

As quick as it appeared, was as quick as it disappeared. Vanished into the dark of night.

"What was that?" Sir Ranald inquired.

"A ghost perhaps." Sir Pompen responded as he teased Ranald for showing signs of fear.

"Enough." a stern Lee spoke.

The boat continued to travel until they all reached their points of execution. No other boats in sight now. They all grew weary, famished, and worrisome.

"Captain Lee, we've been out here for bloody hours, where is the signal, what is the hold up?"

"Your guess is as good as mines. We will wait for commands."

Men onboard the boat tried their best to stay warm and alert. However, more time has passed and still no signals.

Ross began to show signs of hypothermia.

"I'm sorry mate, but it looks like there isn't a signal, and if there is, we missed it. Ross is in shock; can't you see he's in the corner shaking. You must do something, you're in charge, any deaths are on your hands." Sir Pompen expressed.

The men howling their breathes into their hands. Shaking to try and keep whatever warmth they can salvage. All looking to Lee for answers

"This is no mistake, rather a cruel joke, or an attempt on my life. I believe we have been fooled. There is no signal. Men we must dock the boat and head into Village. I will do all the talking. Once inside we split up to see what we could find. Someone take Ross straight to the infirmary." Lee ordered.

Upon tying the boat at the dock. The first thing Lee noticed was a young girl. A strange young girl. She looked like she was lost. Wearing rags for clothes. The look of an abandoned child. A hungry child.

"What are you doing out here close to the waters in this cold air. By yourself?" Lee asked the child.

The little girl, however, did not respond.

"What is your name?"

The little girl stood about. Still as a statue. Biting her fingernails.

"I say we take her and hold her at ransom. She must belong to someone here." Sir Pompen suggested.

"Are you mad? We're not taking a little girl as hostage."

The little girl stepped closer towards the men. In reaction, some of the men deployed their weapons.

"Lower your weapons." Lee declared.

"This little girl is strange. She doesn't speak. How do we know if she's not a set up." Sir Pompen asked.

"Look at her. Does she look the least bit dangerous?"

"Maybe not dangerous, but she looks sick."

"We will continue our mission. Leave the girl."

The men headed through the tall wet marsh and crossed over into the main commons. Only to be greeted by the Village leader. Who was backed by man soldiers.

"We come in peace. Sent by Leader Mary-Ann of blue, to find her daughter. She went missing yesterday. Any word?" Lee addressed.

"I assure you there is no missing daughter here. What a pity though. Katianna. So young and beautiful, we the people hope for her safe return." Jackson, leader of the White Village spoke.

"So, you wouldn't mind if my men had a look around?"

The two faced each other down.

Jackson stepped aside and extended his hand for passings.

"Of course not. Our home is your home. Please check around, ask around. Warm up, get a bite to eat and be on your way. We have nothing to hide."

Lee and his men did just that. Walking through the Village, one of the men spotted the same little girl from the water.

Suspicion risen, however they proceeded to focus on the task.

They walked through every inch of that Village three times over and found no signs of Katianna. They spoke to the people. Nothing.

Growing frustrated Lee refused to stay and eat, warm up, or do anything comfortably. For what is a happy man without his happy lady.

Ross was in further need of urgent care and was not able to return to the boat with the others. That meant leaving him behind.

"I assure you Lee of Bamburgh-Blue your man will be safe here. We will send word of his progress, and he will return home as soon as his health allows." Jackson reassured.

Doubtful as he may be. Lee must move on to explore other leads. Before untying the boat, Jackson and his people stood about, In the back of and far off to the side was the little girl once more.

Drifting away through the waters, Lee and this very dainty little girl locked eyes completely.

It appears as though the little girl knew something. Either that or her silent stares were a cry for help. Either way something was off-putting.

When the boat reached a far enough distance out of sight. Lee did something instantaneously strange.
"Nigel." Lee called to him quietly.
"Yes Sir."
"I need a favor mate. I have reason to believe there's more to be found in Alfriston (White). My spirits are discerning. I want you to take the boat back home. Tell no one of my plans."

"But Sir, you cannot go off alone. What's to become of you, and what will I tell Mary-Ann."

"Tell Mary I got lost in the woods, make up something and stick to it. I will never forgive myself if I did not act on my gut feeling. If I am wrong, I will retreat immediately."

"Why me Sir?"

"Because next to me, I know your knowledgeable in steering boats."

"Godspeed my brother." Nigel shook Lees hand.

Moments after Lee told the men aboard that he must rest a bit and put Nigel in charge.

He then walked to the back of the boat. Pretending to rest and waited for everyone to sleep or become occupied before he simply fell off the back of the boat.

Surprisingly no one noticed. The sounds of the rough waters overpowered the sound of him dropping. There would only be a matter of time before one would notice.

EIGHT
KATIANNA

The further into the woods I ran the more regret I felt. Maybe if I turn back now, I can salvage some of this chaotic mess, but then there was a piece of my mind that told me to keep going and be free as I'd wish.

After a while, I grew restless. Thus, stopping at a shrubbery looking tree stump.

"Stupid, Stupid." I said to myself as I hit the palm of my hand against my forehead.

"Do you always talk to yourself and tell yourself your stupid?" A Strangers voice shadowed from behind me. With a strange accent unfamiliar to me.

My heart raced as I immediately jumped looking for anything I could use as a weapon.

"Stay back, I will hurt you." I said while slowly walking backwards.

This stranger laughed so hard; it made me angry.

"What do you think is so funny? Who are you? Why are you here?"

"You're a strange girl. You come to my home and interrogate me. I should be the one asking all the questions?"

"Home? You live on a tree stump?"

"Are you mad little lady. Maybe you are a crazy. Of course, I don't live on a tree stump. However, this is my area and have been so for years."

We both stood there staring at each other up and down. As I do not pose him a threat, I will not let my guard down.

"What is your name?" I asked.

"What is your name?" he asked.

"Where are you from?" I asked.

"Where are you from?" he asked.

"Stop that immediately."

"You stop it."

This stranger is very annoying. He looked like he hadn't bathed in days, yet he looked extremely fit. Quite a handsome man.

Long black hair that faded into a lighter brown shade towards the ends. He had a full stubble and wore his hair in a bun. Light green almost grey looking eyes.

Geesh I'm beginning to think I'm obsessed with eyeballs. His shoulders are broader than most. Full lips, and a slanted small scar that stretched across the top and bottom of his right eye, as if someone or something came close to scratching his eye out.

"I'm not here for trouble. I just wanted to rest a bit. Catch my breath, I'll be on my way." I stated.

"Catch your breath from what? What's a girl like you doing so far out here, alone?"

"That is none of your business."

"Perhaps it's not, but you're the one that is displaced not me. Either you're running from something or running towards something. Either way, you need help."

"Oh, and what am I supposed to seek help from you? I don't know you, maybe your some sort of freak or monster. Maybe you're the one who takes ladies and sacrifices them for blood in the woods. Are you a heretic?"

"Maybe I am, and maybe I'm not. You can take my help, or you can starve to death and fight off animals all by yourself. I'll have you know there are wild boars nearby."

"I'll take my chances."

I began to run away with no direction or certainty.

"Ok your choice. Be safe Katianna." Stranger yelled to me.

Instantly causing me to stop in my tracks and slowly walk back towards him.

"You know who I am?"

"Of course, I do, everyone does" he said as he bowed before me in a sarcastic gesture.

"What do you know of me."

"I know your next in line, and that's all I need to know."

"What guarantee can you give me that you will not kidnap me?"

"You have my word." He extended his hand.

Reluctant to take his hand. However, I was tired, hungry and cold.

"I will go with you for a moment just long enough for food and warmth, then I'm leaving. If you try anything funny, I swear to God."

The stranger laughed yet again.

"I'd hate to break it to you; you're not kidnapping material. Besides I know your mother and I know your stature. I think I'd like to keep my head on my body."

Off we went as I followed him through the back trails of the woods and into a small cottage surrounded by traps.

One would assume an escapee or a person with many enemies lived here. The first thing I noticed upon entry was many swords hanging near the front door.

A lit fire in the fireplace, a few primitive lamps, and a bunch of small carved wooden structures that represented that of a Childs toy.

"What are these?" I said whilst holding one.

As quickly as I touched one was as quickly as he snatched it away.

"Do not touch my belongings unless you ask."

"Apologies. I didn't know you were sensitive about your toys."

"They're not toys, they are crafted sculptures I make with my bare hands."

"There are so many of them, they're quite amazing, what talent you must have to make these. So……. detailed." I said while examining the sculptures.

Seemingly annoying this stranger. May it be wise to shut up and stop touching things.

We continued to walk towards the back. Passing a room with a locked door.

"This room is where you can rest."

"Charming." I added while looking around at the smallest darkest room with one quilt on the floor. However, beggars cannot be choosers.

"I will fix you a hot meal."

"Thank You."

Hours passed before I'd waken. Jumping out of my sleep, not remembering that I fell asleep in the first place.

There was a bowl on the floor next to me. One of the lamps was lit, and I was covered with a quilt. Curiosity leads me out the door.

There he was, sitting at the fireside, carving yet another sculpture.

"Sleep well?" he asked.

"I suppose so. I didn't realize how exhausted I was."

"Fifteen minutes it took me to make you soup. You were already sleeping when I returned."

Feeling abashed I sat next to him at the fireside.

"You looked so peaceful I did not want to disturb or alarm you." he added.

"Thank You, how kind of you." Peeking over at what he was doing I couldn't help but to ask.

"Are those sculptures for something or someone specific?"

"Something or Someone like who?" he asked.

"I don't know maybe a child, or a wife, a lady perhaps." I responded.

The stranger blushed a little.

"No wife, no lady, no child. It's just something I do for fun, it keeps me busy, a hobby." he replied.

"Oh."

An awkward moment of silence secluded the air.

"You know if you want to ask me anything you can ask me flat out, don't be so subtle."

"Really."

"What is your name."

"I am Thomas. Thomas Walsh."

"Why do you live out here all along?"

"That's a long story."

"Where else do we have to go."

He took moments and sighed before he spoke. Perhaps debating if I was worth telling his story to. Afterall, trust is sacred.

"Years ago, while I was just a boy, men whom nobody had ever seen before, stormed my Village. Killing innocent people including both my parents and little brother. They burned the entire Village. I barely escaped. If not for the help of my mother, I'd be dead too. She hid me in a small closet. Very few of us survived. I don't know much more about the true story. Only rumors. All I remember is being scared in that closet. One of the men found me and put his finger to his lips and closed the door back and shouted to others that it was all clear. He had a beard you could braid, and a scar on his hand that resembled the letter X. That is all I know. I've been on my own ever since."

Stunned and broken hearted from Thomas story, there was an emptiness that filled the air.

"How come you never seeked help over at any of the other Villages?" I asked.

"Help." he laughed.

"How did you survive on your own, how did you eat"?

"Well, I trained myself. I learned to move fast-quickly. I stole from other Villages. I hunted animals. I practically did anything to survive."

I rested my hand at his back.

"Thomas I am so sorry you had to go through such horrible things, and then deal with the aftermath on your own. I feel for you."

We sat in silence as there were no other words left to say. In that moment, even with a stranger, I feel at ease. Finally, a person with a much more tragic history and problems than I, yet one I can relate to in other ways.

"Would you mind if I'd stay a bit longer?" I asked.

"I don't mind at all. You are welcome here for as long as you like. Just remember a Lady of your stature brings about hungry wolves."

I knew exactly what that meant. Time was not on my side.

"You're not lonely out here all alone?" I asked.

"Do I miss the company of others. Sure, but lonely, I am not. I like being alone, no one to distrust. Besides, can't really miss what you barely ever had."

"That is a very frivolous way to live don't you think Sir Thomas?"

"No, I don't think Lady Katianna. I am perfectly happy and fine. Maybe you should tell me what you're running away from instead of questioning why I choose to live the way I live" he responded with irritability.

"That is an even longer story than yours."

"Oh, come on now. Can't be that long. Rather simple actually." he regarded with sarcasm.

"And what of my life do you know." I responded.

"I know you're highly favored. Born into a wealthy family. Spoiled girl who had everything handed to her. Probably ran away because something didn't go her way."

I rose from my seat filled with doubt and anger.

"Shut up, you're a fool. You know nothing about me or my life. How dare you judge me. Just because you grew up as a less fortunate child doesn't mean I'm privileged. I've worked hard for everything I have. I've earned the respect people give me." I yelled and paused while I gathered myself and belongings.

"Coming here was a mistake. Sorry to impose. I'll be on my way."

There I was again. Blood boiling. Questioning my existence and decisions. While Thomas sat there so calm, and unbothered.

"Are you done?" he asked.

"You're a miserable mean man. Maybe that's why you're alone. "Maybe no one can stand to be around you." and with that said I turned to walk away before he grabbed my arm.

"Let go of me immediately." I demanded.

I was in a panic at this point. Feeling threatened. Not knowing who this man is. Maybe he's going to hurt me.

"My apologies my lady. It was not right for me to pass judgement. You're right, I know nothing of your life. Please don't go. Or at least if you must, allow me to escort you to your destination."

The wind blew swaying the leaves was merely the only sound one could hear in tranquility. This Thomas, so incommodious, yet strikingly handsome. Every essence in my soul, curious to say the least.

"Fine I will stay with the exception to a few rules."

"Please continue." he said as he bowed his arm.

"First you must tell no one of my being here."

"Does it look like I have many friends to tell."

"Secondly, I get to sleep by the fire on the paille instead of the dark cold room on the floor."

"Done." Thomas quickly agreed.

Days turned into nights. Nights turned into more next days. I'm surprised no one has found me. Time passing as simply as the color yellow.

I've gotten to learn much about Thomas during my stay with him. As he did I. He is guarded, yet a protective man. A patient man. Very spiritual and cunning, but also Cynical and meticulous.

Most importantly a man of his word. He took his time to make me feel comfortable. Delicate to my feelings. He even helped me train agility. My heart, although every day in hiding thought of Lee every night before sleep. A now confused heart.

I've grown fond of Thomas. Even having thoughts of what his lips taste like. I'd be fooling myself if I said I wasn't interested. He came at exactly the right time in my life. He's everything I need at this moment.

However, he is safe. An escape from reality. Although this is what I asked for. Deep in my soul, I know this is not how it ends.

The righteousness that flows through the blood of my veins knows that I must go back and face my Village. I must take my place. I cannot hide forever.

I planned on giving word to Thomas of my departure to return to Village tonight. My hope is that he will join me and take a place in the Village. He is not someone I can simply forget.

As I await his return from fetching pails of water and whatever catch that will be dinner. I laid there. Missing touch.

Closed my eyes and let my mind take me places. Touching my own breast, sliding fingers across my lips. Inserted my fingers in my mouth to transfer spit. First, I traced my nipples with my wet fingers, while they hardened from the kisses of air.

Then I Placed my fingers on my clit and rubbed up and down until all the juices dripped down my thighs. Moaning while I continued rubbing, going faster. Ready to release.

Before I could release, I opened my eyes and there he was. Thomas. Standing there. Shirtless. Quietly watching me. Enjoying the sight of me pleasuring myself. Seeing him turned me on further, as the sight of him only made me want to keep going. So, I did.

His strong stance, muscles bulging, the sweat dripping from his chest as it curved around every crevice of his body. I looked him in his eyes while I moaned and continued to touch myself. I wanted to break him. Till he could take it no longer just watching me. Till he came to touch me.

He walked over to me and fell to his knees. He took my fingers and inserted them in his mouth so he could taste me. He leaned into me kissing me gently.

Tasting my own juices off his tongue. Sweet. I wanted him so badly to penetrate me. As I could clearly see he was rock. He wanted it too, but instead he took his fingers and touched for me.

He swiped up the dripping juices to keep the wetness while he stroked his fingers in a circular motion around my clitoris, hearing me moan louder and louder, kissed me again, just as I was about to release, he whispered to me. "Open your eyes." He demanded. "Look at me."

"Why?" I opened my lustful eyes to meet his green grays. Our eyes locked. Mines growing watery from emotion.

"So, I can see your soul when it leaves your body." He continued "You're so Beautiful……..come for me." He whispered.

Never breaking eye contact while he went faster and faster, watching me squirm and biting my lips. Whimpering to his touch. I released. So hard all over his fingers.

He didn't stop until I calmed down. Then he took me in his mouth to taste all the juices as if he had to make sure he drained it all from my clitoris. Sent me crawling up the lounge begging him to stop.

When the moment was over. Thomas held me in his arms. He let me stay in his arms for as long as I needed to be there.

The weirdest thing happened. I cried. I cried so hard, I screamed. All the while he would not let me go. I felt as if he allowed my burdens to unload into him. He played softly in my hair while I cried.

Thomas saw me. Saw me when I felt invisible.

"It's ok. I got you. I see you. You can cry." he said.

NINE
LEE

ΩHITE ϛIΛΛAΓ
(WHITE VILLAGE)

The people here are weird. A village so close, yet so different.

All the women seem to be branded with a seal that represents the number 3 on their hands. The men heavily armored. As if they await a war at any given moment. No one here seems to be living, only alive.

Soulless, sadden, serious, somber. There is darkness here. Not like back home where the people are happy. Smiling every day. Gaudy within.

The goal is to look for the girl from the waters. She knows something. The walls just inside the entrance to the Village are painted black. Strangely enough.

Much different than I remembered it to be when we first looked here. The pillars are marked with red, also in the number three. The red being that of blood. Some dried and old. Some fresh and new.

Whatever weird and dark entities that lies within the walls of this Village will not be forsaken on behalf of Katianna.

I found a black shawl to cover myself with to fit in. I mustn't be noticed. However, to fit in I must become a goth. As that seems to be the way there. Black. Dark.

I grounded up black dirt from the grounds and marked my face beneath my eyes. Then my arms. Dirty is the way.

Perhaps the people here don't bathe. Perhaps there isn't much running water to do so. Wanting to turn back, however a task to uphold Simultaneously.

As I lurked around, I overheard of an event that was to take place that night near the burrows onside the willow tree. I must quickly learn those coordinates. As this Village is twice the size of Blues.

My best bet is to find a servant and gain as much information as possible.

Continuing to wander about until I stumbled upon the kitchen. Leaving the swinging doors was a young man carrying a tray of food.

I followed him to see where the tray was headed. It landed in a chamber near the front gates. Perhaps the Chambers of the Village leader.

I Waited until the young man began walking back to the kitchen before gaining speed to catch up enough close behind.

"Exciting day."

The young man looked in my direction with confusion. I'm sorry, do I know you?" the young man replied.

"Does anyone ever truly know each other? The names Lee, what's your mate?"

"Servant number 3." he smiled, knowing he was speaking in sarcasm.

"Oh, come on, I'm sure your mother didn't give you that name at birth."

"As I am just as sure your mother didn't raise you to pry."

"I'm not prying, I'm merely getting acquainted."

"I'll tell you one secret. Change your pattern if you're trying to fit in, you have the scent of an outsider." servant 3 replied. He then vanished into the halls leaving me behind.

The new tactic is to charm one of the ladies. An affectionate heart is a portal to an open soul. All I had to do was catch a bird with salt on its tail. However, there are many flocks.

Besides, how will it be easy to pretend long enough to charm someone when the heart is enamored. To deceive is just as bad as the actual act within itself. What needs to be done will be done, and so to set off to cover ground looking for the perfect catch.

Praying amongst many (all ladies) in the common grounds of the Village, was a very beautiful, pale skinned, blonde curly hair lady. Who locked eyes with me as I slowly walked by. Knowing she was the one. Waiting for the right moment to pounce. Waited in the wings.

Walking about alone, I grabbed her from the crowd.

"A woman who prays is like a butterfly who just earned its wings."

"I suppose so." She replied. She spoke in a deep British accent.

"Spare time to tell me more?"

"What, have you never prayed before?" She responded curiously.

"Of course, I have. Just not as pretty as you looked doing so."

Her cheeks turned red.

"Is that a regular smile, or a blush? There's a difference you know."

"Really, do explain."

"I will as soon as you stop walking so fast and slow down long enough."

And so, she did just that. She stopped in place.

"A regular smile is fake. Something you do to be polite. Like when someone makes a terrible joke, and it didn't land but you don't want to be rude. But a blush, a blush is when your cheeks go so high up it leaves heat.

That heat turns red. Now that's when its real and a person is intrigued. Correct me if I'm wrong."
She paused, staring at Lee with her arms folded.
"What is your name?" she asked.
"Brennon."
"And yours?" Lee asked.
"Lily"
"A beautiful name for a beautiful girl."

Lily once again not being able to stop it. Blushed incoherently.

"And she blushes yet again" I extended my hand for her to place hers in mines, and so she did.
"Nice to meet your acquaintance, Lily."

We walked wherever she wanted to go. I had no direction. I knew getting close to her would lead me to the answers I needed to know.

At this point. It's my only option.

BAYE ɕIΛΛΑΓE

Back home in Blue. The Village was in a shambles. As everyone scratched their heads. Mary-Ann and Joe holding countless and sleepless meetings with the men who returned from search. Especially from the boat in which Lee led.

"No one will be rested until my daughter is found." The leader spoke aggressively.

She stood up yet again to assert dominance and fear to the people.

"Someone, anyone explain to me again how not only was there no succession, but how a captain of one of the boats simply vanished into thin air?"

"I'll wait, we have all day." The leader said as she sat back and sunk into her chair.

Everyone too afraid to speak. Everyone's either looking at each other, or staring at the walls, or in the air. Looking for unimaginable answers to fall from the ceiling. The Black Knight at Mary-Ann's side (still) stepped forward.

"Time is not on our side here. If no one comes forward, I will ask of consequences to take play. It is the only way to get the people talking." He looked to the leader for her blessing, as sure as she gave it to him.

"We will start stripping your lands, sending people to exile. Furthermore, if you are suspected of foul play, you

will be taken to the hole, until your name can be cleared, and if your name is not cleared. Execution."
Everyone started gasping and sighing. Some even cried.

"With all due respect, that is rather harsh, as I am sure there is a better way. Less extenuating perhaps." Sir Nigel suggested.

The people were shocked by his response. Thus, slowly separating themselves from the left and right of his sides.

How audacious of Nigel. The Black Knight shooting looks of anger. Called to Nigel front and center.

"Everyone look upon this man as a good sign, because of him, you all have more time before it is you who will be in his place, but for now, being so brave, he will be first to be taken to the hole."

Everyone gasped while they stood there and looked about.

"The hole? Why must I be taken to the hole. I've done nothing wrong." Nigel pleaded as Mary-Ann summoned guards to take him by force. Nigel of course, resisted. Thus, leaving them no choice but to drag him along the way.

"Would anyone else like to volunteer?" He looked about in the crowd.

"You?" He pointed "You? He pointed.

Everyone cowering in corners and taking steps back. "My thoughts exactly."

The gathering was to be dismissed for the time being. However, no one was to leave the Village or even be near the gates. They were restricted and given orders to shelter in place. Anyone caught would be immediately implicated.

Mary-Ann called in favors to other Villages for help, with whom she has strong Alliances. Clearly the power of her Village alone was not enough.

She called on Black, which would be a given, and also to green. Mary-Ann certainly have made some enemies during her leadership.

Some Villages won't be so eager to aid her. It was said that she's broken treaties with Brown and Yellow years ago during a trade gone wrong.

Every year they come to the BlackField festival wanting to trade fox fur for wood. Yellow left shorthanded each time, and Brown always treated like the black sheep. Unwanted, unsavory.

Boats docked from black and green as they joined together. Green is with great company of the Purple Village, thus Purple joining.

"Tonight, we end this. Tonight, we fight. Tonight, we find her and bring her home." The leader declared while everyone cheered.

Commotion abrupt when the bearer of the gates is opened, and The Village gets ambushed while Mary-Ann is giving speech. Men were stumbling everywhere. Women and children, running to safety. Horses ransacking throughout the Village.

"This is an ambush. Slaughter whomever is not with us. There is a traitor amongst us." Mary-Ann shouted. Drawing her own sword.

The intruders knew exactly the right time to ambush. They knew exactly how to cover ground. They even knew of the broken bridge near the tunnel that led through to the back entrance.

No one ever seeks passage there. It has been blocked off for some time. It was as if they had a blueprint. There was no way anyone beside residents, would have known the entire layout.

Not even the people who have lived in Blue since birth knew every nook and cranny. The Village was surrounded. It seems that the Villages who were not willing to aid, were the same ones joining force to take Blue down.

They proposed a willing defeat or a showdown. Children were ripped from their mothers' arms. Ladies were taken as hostages.

Torches were set to cottages. Men were wounded. As most, were not equipped for war. Only having one sword each. Some, having nothing at all.

The Mother declared that she would never surrender. Arrows were deployed into the air facing warriors of Blue.

Mary-Ann quickly used her power to stop the arrows midair. Forcing a turn around. Unfreezing them at the moment it pointed directly back above the enemies' heads.

Not one of them paid attention enough to even notice. They were all so viciously avid. Eyes popping, foaming at the mouth, and marching forward with purpose. They've come for blood.

Until half their men were taken down. Either having been killed or injured severely. Cyrus, the leader of Black, channeled his power of earth manipulation to grab and bound as much men as he could at their feet and hands, tying them up with the strongest vines.

Squeezing at them like a snake do its prey, until it sucks the life out. Zenobia, the leader of Yellow counteracted with her aerokinesis power to summon the air.

Whirling the wind at over seventy miles per hours before throwing it towards Cyrus. Causing him to release his hold on her people.

Most did not survive the grip of his force. Cyrus and all those near him were knocked several feet away from battle.

Some landing so hard, their skulls broke. Some went straight off the cliff, falling hundreds of feet to their death. Mary-Ann froze Zenobia and several people around her.

However, she could not hold them frozen, and still fight. Or hold them frozen while trying to freeze again, until she unfreezes the first set.

So, she focused on channeling her powers to its fullest. Which could ultimately lead to death, the longer they stayed frozen.

Eventually it would become too much to bear, and their bodies would disintegrate.

Meanwhile The Black Knight, the skillful swordsman that he is, took the lives of many. Fighting alongside Joe. Decapitating heads in swifts' movements. The leader of brown. Arias channeled his powers by turning red until his body was ablaze. Spat fire out with his mouth and hands. Many fell to ash and dust within the blink of an eye.

Mary-Ann grew weaker the more she left her signet flowing. Her body shaking, ready to give.

"Nowwww." She called to Gabriel, leader of Purple.

The ground shook. Causing many to jump across broken pieces of the earth beneath them. Gabriel's body turned into a sparkly blue.

Water rose from beneath the mountains. Mary-Ann urged her side to take cover. They well all aware of what was to come when she ordered Gabriel to go.

High tides of water swept through the entire field. Mainly at Arias. Taking down his blaze. Drowning him in the waters as it washed it away.

"Retreat…. retreat." Zenobia ordered. Calling back everyone from her army. Mary-Ann taking heath to Zenobia clearly being the orchestrator.

Victory is ours. This time.

ELEVEN

LEE

ΩHITE ςIΛΛΑΓE

It's been a few days since I've pretending to be a White Villager. I can't believe it's even been this long.

I assumed Katianna would return once she calmed down.

My faith in her, strong, but I'm beginning to grow worried. It hasn't been easy avoiding being caught by the leader, or his daughter.

I'm not sure how much longer I can keep this up. They'd know right away who I was.

Lily informed me of all she knows without even realizing she was just a girl who's fond of a man and spilling secrets. In order to get her secrets, I had to pretend to like her, to laugh at her dry jokes.

Every moment I had to pretend to lust for her was another moment I had to counter. She led me to the exact location of a sacred event that originally was supposed to take place the first night I got here.

Night fell. I blended in as best I could. The Village leader spoke in a weird tongue. One I've never heard before. I tricked Lily into believing I knew by playing along and saying the wrong things knowing she'd correct me. The rest was spoken in English.

"We must strike again while they are weak. We must capture and kill their next in line. We can then take over, become a stronger Village. Convert those who are willing, dispose of those who are not." Jackson spoke vaguely.

The Villagers stood about wearing white masquerades. Holding crosses near their chest. Amongst them. Lady Willow, daughter of Jackson. This night was hers. Once all the plans set out in victory. Lady Willow was to complete her challenge and take place as the new Village leader.

"My people, give me your loyalty, give me your prayers. And tonight, I will lead you to conquest."

Villagers from White chanted and danced. Spirits taken over their bodies.

"Does that mean war?" I asked pretending to be confused.

"Don't be silly Brennon, after the sacrifice, they will get her."

"Get who?"

"Katianna."

My heart dropped at the mentioning of her name. Realizing that their plan all along was to ambush Blue, find Katianna and kidnap her.

My suspension of this Village having something to do with her disappearance is validated. They couldn't possibly have had those plans if they already had her captive. Perhaps they only learned of her being missing when we came before looking.

There was no doubt in my mind that we tipped them off. Spotting the little girl from the waters wandering near the woods away from the meeting. I slowly crept off to catch her.

"Hello." saying it delicately as to not scare her off while threading lightly. The girl is mute. "What's your name?" The girl started humming. "Are you lost? Do you have parents here?" The girl shrugged "I can help you if you like" I pulled out a scone from my bag and handed it to the girl. She snatched it immediately.

I continued to walk near her as the girl kept going. "I'm looking for my friend. Have you seen a woman here you never seen before?" Or a man who came here ill from another Village." The girl prances around. Just as I was ready to give up.

"I've seen your friend. She hides with the man in the woods." My feet quickly running back to her.

"Where?" I pleaded desperately. The girl pointed across the river.

"Can you tell me what she looks like?"

"She is pretty."

Not much help. "Anything else you can tell me."

The girl stopped. With her back towards Lee. In a solid quiet stance. "She comes out sometimes. She runs with him."

"Runs with him. Like what? Trying to run away from him?"

"No, runs like they are racing. She is happy. She runs with the wolf" The girl bends over to pick flowers from the ground.

More confused than I ever was to begin with. No longer sure if this girl is speaking of Kati at all.

"Runs with the wolf. What wolf? What are you speaking of? Will you show me? Please? … if you show me, I will get you anything you want." My desperate pleas sparking interest in her eyes. I seem to have hit a spot.

"Can you give me a mom, and a dad?" her face grew saddened.

"Perhaps not exactly, but I can guarantee you comfort and stability in Blue. The people there will welcome you. You'll be praised as a hero once they learn you're the one responsible for leading me to their leader."

The girl walked in the direction of the waters. Assuming it was her acceptance to my proposal, my steps trailed behind hers like any newborn cub to their parent.

BAYE ςIΛΛAΓE

Back home Villagers were fighting for their lives. Many were slaughtered on both sides. The Village was nearly burned down.

Thankfully with the help of Black and Green, we've succeeded this time. However, many weeping wives covered in their husband's blood.

Leader of Blue graciously agreed to build a shrine to sanctify the site where lies the lost men.

People gathered in the common awaiting instructions.

"My good people. Those who fought till their dying breath, those who were brave. This was an act of hatred. Catastrophic diplomatic senseless violence. There will be vengeance and we will rise again." Mary-Ann gave speech. The people cheered on aggressively angered.

"We will train, everyone here must learn a skill. We would have been more successful than we were. Make no mistake, we will prevail until we see more blood of thy enemies than we have of our own. I would like to personally show my gratitude to our ally Villages of Black and Green who fought alongside us. We are forever in your debt."

The people began chanting and praying. The Mother was taken away as she appeared to be lightheaded.

"Are you ok dear." Joe comforted his wife as she coughed up blood when they retreated to their chambers.

"I'll be fine Joe. We must find her quickly before the people start to question our reign. She must take her place. She is ready, I can feel it. We need her."

While she recovered spending time in her chambers aided by David, who mixed her many potions that he claims comes directly from the earth.

Joe led control of The Village reassuring the people they are safe and protected. He broke people down into groups, pending their strengths and weaknesses.

While The Black Knight orchestrated soldiers from his Village along with Green, to set out when the night fell.

Purple was to accompany them at once. However, Purple seemingly fell off the Grid.

Whispers in the night are secrets in the walls. A Village torn. Catastrophe. The very reason there are leaders. The strength of the leader determines the fate of the people.

One must be strong, smart, and brave. Willing and ready to risk their own life for the sake of their people.
"Joe." A sick Mary calls to her husband
"Yes dear." he rushed to aid her at bedside.

"I am weak, I have been sick for some time now. I need you to do me a favor" holding her head Joe assures his wife that he'd do anything for her.

She whispers to him "Implement Lee for our daughter's disappearance. Kill him."
Joe jumps, frightened by his wife's request.
"That is Sin."

"Every sin weighs heavy Joe. Every sin can be weighed against an act of faith. Grow the faith and the sin is diminished."

"Mary-Ann, my love. What do you speak of? Please don't speak that way. For do you not know the souls who sin are the ones who will die a double death the day of reckoning."

A confused Joe merely recognizing his wife as his own. His eyes widened.

The Mother drifted off to sleep from a potion David had given her just moments before.

When Joe finally catches up to David. It was sure to be an unpleasant visit.

"Whatever you're giving my wife, end it. NOW." An angry Joe shouted at David as he lunged at him grabbing him by the collar.

"Sir, I assure you, what I give your wife is pure healings from the earth. It is only meant to make her better. Aid her sleep."

Joe spit on the floor before David. A gesture in disgust. "Nonsense, whatever you give her is making her worse. This is a warning, if I find that you disregard my commands, you will pay the price with your life." ......" That is a promise, not a threat."

Peace demolished in the matter of a split second. Worlds collide within the matter of days, war wages within the matter of weeks.

All at the hands from actions caused by one, not many. Katianna, clueless to all that took place in her absence. Wreckage becomes Blue. A leader in a weak state.

The men set out once again. This time with a bigger army, a stronger one. The nights air more frigid than usual. Thus, causing food and supplies to be scarce. Livestock to perish.

THIRTEEN
LEE

Miles away we trailed through the woods. Frost bit fingers cracked and bleeding lips. To survive this, seems nearly impossible, but if ever a chance to find my Love, is a chance of death I was willing to take.

"Hey, aren't you cold? I mean I'm freezing my ass off and you're trailing along unbothered. You don't even have enough layers to keep you warm."

The girl doesn't respond. We continued to walk in silence, up the hills, around the waters, and through the woods. Until we seen a cottage with a dim light. The girl stops.

"There." she points to the cottage.

"There? As in, she is in there?"

The girl shakes her head yes.

"Are you afraid?" I ask. She'd stopped in her tracks.

"Not afraid, this is where I leave you. My journey ends where your destiny begins."

"Leave? Why? don't you want to come to Blue?"

The girl silently walked away. "What does that even mean, your journey ends where my destiny begins?" I shouted and watched as she, yet again, disappeared into the night.

The closer I got to the Cottage, the more nervous and anxious my body grew. Not knowing what I'd find beyond the doors.

Abrupt noises startled me. Leaving me to quickly hide behind a tree. A tree that faced the direction of a side window. An unsheltered window.

My eyes were drawn to the site of Katianna being held in the arms of a man I've never seen before. A feeling so unexplainable.

I watched as the man held her, then covered her up with a quilt before he left out the back door and rode out on his horse.

She seemed sad, and that made me angry. I Watched her as she sipped tea and read from a paper. The noises around me stood still, failing to notice men moving about.

Closing in on the Cottage. The men wore royal coats of arms. Upon realizing the men were not from Blue, I realized this was an attempt on her life.

Instinctively I drew weapons raging at whoever was in path. A surge of adrenaline took over as I pierced my sword through the hearts of those I could reach.

Throwing daggers at those who were further in distance. However, many made it through. Outnumbered, I had no choice but to draw back.

A quick plan to sneak in through the back and save her became a quick plan of defeat. There were no signs of Katianna.

The men left empty handed. My eyes saw nothing that indicated they captured her. Maybe she's hiding or escaped.

I thought to myself. I'd wait for the coast to clear before checking. From what I gathered from one of the men was that "She got away. Perhaps into the woods. She couldn't have got far." Yaa.

The men set off pulling on their horse's bridle. Others ordered to stay back.

Unfortunate luck for those who had. I quietly scanned the cottage, being carefully eagle-eyed. I may not have known who the man was, but if I knew Katianna, I knew there was more to behold within the naked eye.

My sword swayed across the wooden floors as I listened for shallow creaks, drowning out the soft meadows of burning flames. A hollow point reached upon my sword. There lies secrets in the ground.

****

A secret passage one would never find unless they built it themselves. However, a sword so powerful in its findings.

I followed the passage all the way until it led me to an opening above ground. An opening that covered in tall grass in the middle of the woods.

Searching about following the trail of two sets of footprints, led me to Katianna and the man drinking water by the river.

"Drop your weapon." I demanded as I captured him from behind.

"I have no weapon."

"Do not play games with me, I know you hold her against her will, drop your weapon."

"I hold no one against their will, and my weapons are over there laid on the ground by the rocks."

I walked him near his pointed location.

Katianna ran towards us when she made out what's happened.

"Lee, no" she pleaded to me. "He is not of danger, he is not an enemy, he helps me."

"Help you? Katianna, I know that mustn't be true. Do not fear, I am here now."

"Lee, I promise I am telling no tale, it is true, he helps me. Please release him."

Upon realizing she was not covering for him, I let him go. He quickly possessed his weapons.

"What is this?" I asked.

"Long story to explain."

I hate the way she has a hold on me. Even with the rage I feel all over my body, when I look in her eyes, I am still a fool who folds to the power of her beauty.

"Explain then. Humor me as to what this is, while you are out here having the time of your life your Village is physically ill worrying about you, your Village attacked, yet you're here with him, who is this man."

"Village attacked? what do you speak of" she grew worried and anxious.

"Blue was attacked. I was not there; however, in my quest to find you, I hid in White and learned many things. There is an attempt on your life. They planned on capturing you and taking over Blue."

Tension grew as the air thickened.

"We must go back immediately. I have to save my people. I must take my place." She gathered what little belongings she had left.

No explanation given. As if the question I asked about her and this strange man meant nothing to her. Her behaviors off.

Certainly, there's a story. One she's clearly in no mood to tell.

FOURTEEN
KATIANNA

"Thomas, will you join me? I beg of you." My eyes desperately pleaded.

Something that I'm not too keen on. Mother has always told me, women like us should never beg. I'm not above it at this moment. I'd beg the Gods themselves, if it meant helping my people.

Lee watched in confusion as the women he loves, begs another man for his company. It hurts me to hurt him, but there's no time for emotions.

"I will join you long enough until you are safe and then I will go." Those words. So simple, yet so cogent. Maybe I'm in my head too much. Maybe he didn't mean it the way it came off.

"Katianna, what is your relationship to this man?" Lee asked angrily. Tugging softly at my arm.

"There is no time for questions, I promise to explain later. Right now, we must go." His reaction displeasing. It hurts me to see the hurt in his eyes. The same look he gave me the day TBN danced with me. Giving the urgency of the situation, he backed down none-the-less, but I knew it would be far from over.

We set off into the woods. A long journey beholds.

Lee was annoyed on his travels with us. Seeing our bonded connection saddened his heart.

Although I was happy to see him as well. I held him for what felt like an eternity. Thomas watched. Equally annoyed and Jealous.

"Tell me, what has changed since I've been gone?"

"Just as I said people are sick with worry, your mother ordering everyone around, sending people to the black hole for answers. Things are scarce, everything has changed."

"I am stricken with guilt. Had not been for my coward and selfish decisions, things would be different."

"Perhaps, but do not blame yourself, you did what you felt in your heart to do at that moment. The attack was to happen with or without your presence. Maybe even worse with."

"How do you know all of what has happened if you were not there?"

"I paid a spy for information. He is a good man, he kept on his word."

"Hmm, I see, do you think the people will forgive me?"

"I know they will. When we reach, speak to them from your heart, they will accept and love you as they always have."

Lee grew silent. "Tell me what you're thinking. Something is troubling your mind."

"Even after what has happened and all the time that has passed, you still know me well Princess." We shared a laugh. More like a chuckle.

"We lost many lives during the attack. People you once knew can be gone now."

We stared at each other in an unspoken understanding. "Like whom?"

"I am not privy to say. I only got word of many lives lost. Not specific names. I will learn of it just as you.... when we get home."

My heart sunk into my chest. The low blow of horror douching me with its presence.

Dark of night depleted our journey back to Village. We've been traveling for hours.

My legs grew heavy, my vision blurred from sleepy eyes. If I continued any further, I would be nothing more than dead weight.

We rested underneath the redwoods. What was supposed to be a quick rest stop suddenly turned into a dream. That dream interrupted by the sounds of crunching leaves from quiet feet.

My mouth was covered by the hand of Thomas upon waking. I screamed into his hands. He beckoned. The way he did back at the cottage when we were ambushed.

A gesture I was all too familiar with. I slowly crept to a deep sleeping Lee, kicking softly at his leg with my foot until he gained conscious for me to beckon him. Immediately he became aware of the dangers we were facing.

We watched at a safe distant, hidden, while men ransacked our camp.

"We must go." Thomas alerted quietly.

Before we had a chance to fully escape, we were met with the sword of two men. We were surrounded. They must have come from behind the willows.

We drew swords quickly. Lee killing one, Thomas killing the other. I fought with my life as two men rushed me, sweeping me off my feet.

I managed to prod a dagger into the neck of one of the men. He quickly dropped to the ground holding his neck. The other hitting me so hard in the face, I'm sure something is broken. He threw me over his shoulder like a rag doll.

I watched from a distance as Thomas and Lee fought for their life. I thought about calling out in distress, but I knew that would deter them both.

No more blood will be spilled from my decisions. I kicked, punched, and screamed. Surely not giving up without a fight.

If he's to take me, it won't be an easy task. I bit into his ear hard. His grip suddenly loosened. He sighed in pain. I used the advantage to weasel my way from his grip. Only he was quicker.

His sword placed on my neck, piercing my flesh enough for blood to drip. Defeat consumed me. Nowhere to run. Nowhere to hide.

He whipped me to my knees. Towering over me, he spat on the ground besides me. Speaking in a language unknown to me. It was a weird dialect. Almost Pagan.

I've heard it before when David spoke it with another. This was almost similar, but different. He circled around me slowly. Like I was some trapped helpless animal.

He trailed his sword up and down my body. Stopping at my breasts. "I don't know dear, you're a little too enticing to bring back alive. I may have to go against orders and have you for myself." He bent over behind me. Sniffing in the scent of me.

Nasty sweaty cheek pressed against mine. His stubble so full, all I felt was prickly hairs all over. He opened his mouthed and stuck his tongue out, licking my face from my chin to my eyes.

The scent of something dead lingered on his tongue. It was so vile, I felt sick to my stomach. I spit in his face in discontent. "Coward." I yelled at him. He took my spit from his face with his dirty fingers and put in his mouth. "Mmm, we practically shared a kiss sweetheart." He stated. I grew anxious as I attempted to get up.

He placed the sword on my neck once more. All I could think about was the boys. I hope their ok. They were no longer in my vision, as this coward had me facing the stream.

All I heard was swords swinging, clashing, and panted breathes. Suddenly a wolf appeared. From the left side of us.

The cowards body shifted further out from me. Still with his sword placed on my neck.

I strained to see as much as I could through my peripherals. It had white undercoat. A chestnut, grey, black and white top, leading down to its tail.

A rarity only talked about in fables. The wolf grinned its teeth the closer it got to us.

Licking its tongue over its prodigious teeth. He stood huge, and vicious. The coward gulped in his throat, but never dropping the sword from my neck. The wolf came close to me. Sniffing over me.

The closer it came, the more the coward backed away. Until his sword was barely there. It was merely just the tip at my throat.

I contemplated making a sudden move. This predicament altering my judgement. As it may be one of the worst ones, I've ever been in.

The wolf stepped slowly to the coward, and he took steps back in fear. Finally lifting his sword to turn it on the wolf. I quickly came to my feet to pull a dagger from its sheath.

Death flashed in his eyes as the wolf jumped to attack him. Tearing at him viciously. Blood splattered everywhere. The wolf looked back at me.

I felt no fear. As if he was sent to help me. The boys came running towards me shocked at the atrocity that unfolded before them.

Thomas pulling me away. We ran. Running past their field of battle, men were laid out. Clearly a victory we won. This time.

We ran until our lungs gave out. "Here, drink up." Lee passed me a flask.

"Thank you." I acknowledged after gulping down the water like a thirsty dry throat Lioness. Upon passing the flask back to him, he passed the flask to Thomas. No one could ever say Lee was not the most gracious person they'd ever met.

Even knowing how uncomfortable and jealous he must feel, he remains holy.

We continued our journey, this time not stopping until we reached home. My heart was torn to pieces from a distance, at the mere sight from what was left of Blue.

Surrounding trees and land in ruins. People weeping at the gates. Burn marks and debris from left over fire. A Village that is not so familiar.

When seeing my arrival, The Villagers rejoiced, giving thanks To Gods for my safe return. They were pulling at me while I walked through the Commons.

"Daughter." The Mother and I came face to face.

I, still a little girl at heart, folded into her with unstricken emotions as the tears flew down my face uncontrollably.

For the first time since I was a child. She too, cried tears as she held me in her arms. There was no safer place.

Her strong hold told me everything without words.
"Is Father, Noah and Joe jr ok?"

"They're fine. Father has fought alongside many; the boys have been sent away to safety." She inhaled a deep breath.

"Katianna, some didn't make it, many didn't make it. We must challenge you again tonight so that we can coronate your leadership." she held my face in her hands "You are ready." I knew deep in my heart it was no question.

Rather more a statement that seeked no response. She was telling me, not asking me. For once I felt ready. I nodded my head up and down in her hand accepting my role.

Something has taken over my body. My nerves. My spirit. The Mother looked different. She looked fragile. And all I wanted was to shield her and keep her safe, and finally earn her honor and leisure.

Not just hers, but every single beating heart in my Village. I owe them all. I was ready to lead.

As I stood there at the podium next to father, I ignored all the nerves that tried to nest and take host of my body. I sucked in a deep breath with my eyes closed.

The silence was loud. Not one person whispering. Instead, all eyes on me. I swallowed my fears and spoke from my heart. Not one single word was mine.

"Our home desecrated. Our families, broken. But our faith……..our faith stands tall. We cannot be broken; we will not accept defeat. WE ARE BLUE." A crowd of angry Villagers screamed in rejoice as I gave speech. The father took over as he seen the hesitant glare in my eyes.

"She has come home to Us." The Father shouted. Pointing swords were drawn facing me "It is a sign from the Gods. Your lanterns worked. It brought her spirit back to us. She will pass the challenge and she will lead."

Villagers were chanting surrounding a circle around me. The Mother was nowhere in sight, neither was Stacey or Lee.

Thomas stood at my side with the quick acceptance of The Mother and Villagers when we first arrived, after I told them what role he played in my survival.

As the crowd grew back to its normal stentorian routine, I fell into the background. Slowly making my way to the entrance, near the flood gates.

"Where are you going?" Thomas asked.

"I promise to be back within an hour. Please make yourself at home. Mingle with the people if you will, I will find you." He watched me until I faded into the crowd. For more reasons than one, I feel safe knowing he's here with me.

"Where is The Mother." I asked Lee, who I found outside my chambers.

"She's deliberating with Parliament."

I sighed in relief before about-facing.

"Where are you going?" he asked like he was afraid if I walked away, he'd never see me again.

"To see Stacey, I want to make sure she's ok. I haven't seen her since we arrived."

"Katianna." a soft-spoken desperate plea met my gaze as he held my arm to stop me from walking off in the direction of her chambers.

"What is it? Lee, if you want to talk, we can do so later. Tonight, is one of the biggest nights of my life. I can have no distractions."

It was the silence that told me. The gulp in his throat, the sweat beads that suddenly appeared on the fore of his head. The way he looked at me in sorrow.

"What is it?" without allowing the words to leave his mouth. I hit his chest demanding to know what happened. "Lee.......no no no no no……..please." I begged dropping to my knees.

He joined me at my knees, holding me at my back while I cried and regurgitated. Choking on my own vomit. Snot seeping from my nostrils like a child playing outside in the winter. The pain cut deeper than any swift dagger piercing fresh skin for the first time.

I screamed until there was no sound left. He could do nothing but restrain me as I tried to fight him and escape.

"I'm sorry. I learned of her death only moments ago. I was told she was killed when Blue was attacked."

Those words pierced my ears like someone was trying to bust my eardrums. The sudden pain, excruciating. My heart feeling grief I've never felt before. How could I let this happen. If I'd been there, I would have had her protected.

I sat on the lounge in my chambers. Covered with a quilt. Looking out the hopeless window as I waited for the council meeting.

I'd asked Lee to leave me alone for a moment while I gathered my heart. But the knock at the door proved him incompetent. Only it wasn't him, it was Thomas. I ran to him the moment I saw him.

He held me tight, like he did the night I cried in his arms. He didn't ask about my troubles. I like that about him. He doesn't pry. He's just there for me.

"I will have a room prepared for you. You are under my, and the Village leader protection here." I assured him.

"I am here for you, and you only. I am not afraid and most certainly don't need protection, but it is good to know that I am accepted."

"Very well then. I am to attend a council meeting within the hour. Please don't go to far."

He assured me he wouldn't, and that he'd wait for me and extend his service to me for whatever I needed.

My heart may be broken, but the wrath of rage I will inflict on whomever is involved and responsible for Stacey's death will be far more harrowing than anyone could ever imagine. I will raise hell in honor of her name.

FIFTEEN

KATIANNA

The council meeting is chaotic. As members of the Parliament talked over one another.

Everyone shouting out their opinions and plans. I sat there; it was the first time I sat in on a meeting.

I assumed it was because of the urgency of my completing the challenge and taking place by deadline. There was a moment where I thought this was how council meetings always went.

Most the time, I was envisioning the blood of Stacy's killer dripping down my bare hands. I was consumed with it. So much so, that I made up an imaginary figment of what I thought her killer looked like.

Just so I can have a vivid vision of how I would torture him.

Maybe I'd hang them upside down and inflict tiny slashes all over their body with Stacy's sword and watch as they bleed out.

No, that wouldn't be plausibly painful enough. Maybe I'd have David mix me a special acidic potion and pour it over their face, watching their flesh boil.

Or I could bring in a vicious animal and let it bite off his penis after smearing fresh strawberry jam on it. Emasculate him.

"Katianna." The Mothers snapping fingers broke my daydream. I repositioned myself.

"Sorry mother, what was that?"

"Snap out of it, we need you here. We're asking if you're ready to complete your challenge tonight."

To be honest I had too many emotions to do anything tonight. But I couldn't bring myself to disappoint her. Not the way her eyes are pleading. "Of course." I reassured her.

"Good, then we will continue as planned. This meeting has concluded."

I looked to the left and then to the right of me. All eyes were on me. Especially Mr. Punic's. The Mother nodded her head at me discreetly, telling me that I was to dismiss Parliament. It appears they've already given me the power to rule. Without me having yet to pass the challenge.

Which means, their faith as well as the faith of the Villagers, lie within my hands.

Upon my getting up, I was frozen. The Mother telling me to stay behind with her eyes. For some reason, The Mother and I have a special connection.

An unspoken bond. Maybe it was from the many years, many moods, and many facial expressions I've learned of her. I knew which each one meant.

No words needed to be spoken. The Father, last to exit, kissed her on the hand. Walked to me and kissed me on the forehead. He never took sides. He loved us both equally.

The room grew distant. The silence was louder than actual words. The Mother rose from her seat and took the one next to me.

Whatever it is she wants to discuss, I can tell it will be the most serious of conversations I've ever had with her.

"My child" She spoke softly. Placing her hand on mine.

"You are not becoming, you have become. It is time. The people need you. Your brothers need you. I need you." I finally looked her in the eyes. I've never heard her so sincere. "I've taught you all I know, and the truth is you will lead better than I, better than those before me, and will, those after you. David has told me so. Though I didn't need him to tell me something that I already knew. I am hard on you for a reason. Us leaders, we don't get to be vulnerable, we don't get to make decisions from our hearts. We must always do what's best for our Village. No matter what it may cost us, even if it costs us our own happiness. I know you're fond of Lee and have been since you were a little girl. However, marrying for the benefit of an extremely strong alliance is what we need. The Black Knight. He is that strong alliance."

I pulled my hand away from her. Anger stirring in my blood like the highest blaze from a fire.

"Now I know it's not what you want, but you will grow to love him in time."

"Mother, I am not marrying that man."

The Mother grew impatient. "Now I tried to warn you and let you make the right decision on your way, but you've forced my hand. Child, you will marry him for the sake of our nation. Once you pass challenge, you will be wed."

"So that's it huh? I don't even get a say in my own future. I'm being forced against my will. That is the exact reason why I ran away in the first place. Because of you. You suffocate me. I cannot breathe when I am near you."

"Shut up." The Mother demanded. "This is the way it's been for years. You are no exception to the rules. You will fall in line like everyone else, as I did."

"Well, I respectfully decline. I step down as the next leader. Let another pass challenge and take over. I much rather prefer my freedom."

"You don't mean that."

"Oh, but I do mother. I mean every bit of it."

"Then why have you come back?"

My shoulders rose and fell as I sat back in the chair.

"You clearly came back here because you care. You love the people just as much as I. If not, more. You want to take your place. You know it's the right thing to do. You knew all along the sacrifices it would take to do so. I've never led you into believing anything other than the truth."

"Why can't I lead without marriage. Times have changed mother."

"Why yes. Certainly, it has. However, no one can rule without marriage. This you know. So, tell me, what is the real problem. Is it that boy?"

"He is not a boy, he is a man, and his name is Lee. It's not just about him."

"Oh, but it is dear."

I sighed.

"If not about him, then who. The man you've come back from the woods with. The one that cannot take his eyes off you, attached to your hip like he's your skin. Katianna, please tell me. Have you given one of them your virtue?"

I looked down at the ground. Searching for answers on the floor. "Did you?" She repeated as she yelled.

"No. Of course not. I do not wish to marry a man I do not love."

"We. Don't. Get. To. Love. What don't you understand about that. When I met your father I…"

"I am not you mother." I cut her off. "I am not a sellout."

My face pierced with pain as she struck me. Nearly knocking me out of the chair.

"Don't ever speak that way to me again. You are ordered to do whatever I say. You are betrothed to the Black Knight, and you will be wed. If I see that you are keeping the company of other men. They will have acted against fate and therefore will have committed treason." She rose from her seat and walked towards the door. "And well you know what happens to treasoners. So, tell me how much do you wish to keep him safe."

Silent tears rolled down my face. I hate her. I will never be to my children, the mother she is to me. Never. I will love them and listen.

Stacey is gone. My heart pulls for two different men. I must pass challenge tonight, we are at war with other Villages, and I am to be married to a man of whom I don't even know his real name.

I'd never in my wildest dreams imagine the weight of the world rested on the shoulders of a nineteen-year-old. This nineteen-year-old.

I searched for Thomas as I were to prepare for the challenge. He'd be the only one that could help me practice and calm me at the same time.

I found him in the corners of the Dutch House. Watching the people of Blue. I feel terrible that he looks so out of place. He looks guarded.

His hand placed on the handle of his sword as if he was ready to draw first blood at any moment. He looks even more appealing than he did when I first met him.

I feel ashamed to say the improper harsh look of him turns me on more than him at ease. It suits him better.

"Thomas." I beckoned. There's a secret passage behind the kitchen that leads to a quiet room on the other side of the wall.

Being in his presence makes me nervous. He's the only man I've ever felt that way for. Not scared nervous. Rather more an intimidated nervous.

The kind that you're not sure if your parents will scold you for misbehaving after a fight you've won, or if they'll high five you and tell you what a good job you did at winning.

Mix that with the butterflies of attraction swirling around in the pit of stomach, and that's the one.

He rested his shoulders against the wall. Sighing, as if it was the first time, he was able to breathe comfortably. His hand no longer gripping his sword. His eyes fixated on me.

"It would be a great honor if you would help me train for tonight's challenge." His eyebrows furrowed. "Yes. Tonight. It has already been set. I need you with me." My eyes searched his for answers.

"What did I tell you the first day I met you?"

"You told me I was a privileged girl who annoyed you and touched your things without asking." We shared a smile briefly.

"Not quite." He began walking towards me. My heart races when it senses immediate touch or close interactions.

Only, I did something different. I stayed in place. I did not cower like I normally would have. Instead, I challenged myself with the signals of my body.

Sweat beads were forming on my forehead and hands against my will.

He placed his hand on my face. I immediately sank my face into his touch. "No." he whispered. "I told you; you never have to beg me for anything." He placed his hand around my waist pulling me into him. "Suit Up. Tonight, you will be the lioness I know you can be. So, you better get out there and you better roar."

I whimper to his touch, to his words. I hate it. Hate the way he makes me feel. The way Mother whimpers to only Father. She folds for him.

"There is something I want to say to you. I know this may be difficult, and I know."

"Shhhh." He stops me mid-sentence. "Talk to me after you pass. Right now, the only thing that matters is your mind. Clear it. Rid it of all your negative thoughts. Do you hear me?"

"I hear you."

I suited up and we trained for forty-five minutes before The Father called for me. It was the most short but intense training session I ever had. There was something different about it.

"Katianna." He called to me before I walked off with the guards. "If you feel afraid, or stuck. Just vision it being me and you out there. No one else around. The way we did in the woods."

Somehow those words were calming. I felt a sense of ease. Walking to Father was a silent walk. No one in my path. Not a friendly face in sight. Yet somehow, I felt good. I feel in my spirit that everything will be ok.

Father waited patiently in his chambers. "Sit." He ordered. "Your mother has told me of your displeasure. She told me you wish to not marry. That you threatened to remove yourself of your duties."

"Father, I…"

"Quiet." I've never seen Father so serious. Not with me anyways. "I know this is hard. I know you are young, and you love another. I am not completely opposed to your union with The Black Knight. I'm also not all for it either. I care about your happiness more than you know. Do you remember the day you ran off in the woods behind Lee?"

"Yes Father. I do." I shamefully looked at the ground. Realizing he knew. There was no denying it. If he's bringing it up, it means he'd always known.

"Well, what you didn't know was that I called off the guards your mother sent after you. I knew all too well why you went. I wanted you to have your moment. I wanted you to go after the one you truly loved. Even though I knew it could never withhold. Still, I wanted you to have your happy moment. Even if it was short lived."

"You did that for me father. How'd you know."

"I was young once. I know what it's like. I also know your mother is hard on you, and although she has a weird way of showing it. She loves you dearly."

Tears formed in my eyes as father went on about love. He was torn between the two. The Mother and me. I never thought about how hard this must be for him.

"Being a leader requires sacrifices. I want you to know something. When you pass the challenge tonight, because I have no doubt that you will, I want you to think long and hard if being leader is a sacrifice you're willing to make. Yes, your mother will be let down, I will deal with her. But you." He walked closer to me. Tilting my chin up to lift my head high as he swiped away tears.

"You are so much different than her. You want love more than you want responsibility, and that is ok. But that is your decision to make. Choose with your soul. Let it guide you to the path of your light."

Outside, the commotion grew louder and louder. Father and I walked out to the balcony. Where we saw Lee and The Black Knight with drawn swords. Villagers stood about carrying on, instead of interjecting. I ran as fast I could to stop it, but it was too late.

Their swords swiped at one another as I pleaded with them both to stop. Lee desperately taking more swipes. Tiring himself quicker.

The Black Knight lunged his sword towards Lees chest, missing it by the slightest of inches. Piercing the flesh of his arm instead.

Blood wasted no time dripping out his wound. I screamed in horror. Lee charged at him slipping on what looks like a rock, quickly regaining his composure swiping his sword.

The Black Knight shuffled around in speed, never allowing Lee an advantage. He took his eyes off Lee for a second, looking in the direction of an abrupt loud noise within the crowd.

Lee wasted no time in getting the upper hand, piercing his sword into T-B-N's shoulder. He screeched in pain. Becoming more ire.

I see the shift in his eyes as the anger grew in chest. The foyer now heaving with people. Both men vigorous to the best of their ability. T he eager desire for more blood lingered amongst both swords. I stepped into the circle of fire. Standing between both men. Warning them that if they wish to kill one another, they must go through me.

The Mother appeared and suddenly they were frozen. She looked at me. "Do you see what this has caused. Men fighting to win your heart. I take it, you told Lee the good news. He is now a treasoner for disobeying my orders."

Everyone looked confused. "Told him what?" Father asked.

"Told him that she is betrothed to another, and she is never to keep the company of him again. Or any other men for that matter."

"Mother stop it." My heart felt heavy. My anger felt even heavier. I am so mad, and I am so tired. Enough. "Stop it right now. Unfreeze him."
"Oh, do you dare give me orders now."

"If you don't unfreeze him and leave him alone. I will step down." Her eyes gazed at mine. "Bad enough I am to marry another by force, you will not take away my friends as well. Because if I must choose between him and to lead this Village. I will choose him, and you will have lost me for good."
"You will do no such thing."

"Try me." I gave her the same eyes she's given me over the years. The ones that speak louder than actual words. The ones that shows the power behind them. I was bluffing, but I certainly mastered the art of my stance. She believed me, and so, unfreezing Lee.

I grabbed him and ran off. We stopped far enough when we were alone. I ripped a piece of cloth from my top, wrapping it as tight as it would go around his wound.

"Lee, you have to stop this. She will have you exiled. Or worse."

"Well, that's just a chance I am willing to take."
He stared at me with such hope.
"Lee, please stop. I beg you. I will never be yours."

His brow furrowed. He walked towards me. Slow but strong striding steps. He kneeled before me.

"Tell me. Tell me that you meant what you said back there. When I was frozen, I was still able to hear. You told your mother that you would choose me. So, choose me. Fight for us. Please."

I could no longer bear looking down on him. The tears were already making its bed in my house.

He rose from his knees and placed my face in his hands. The way Thomas did before he trained me one last time.

Only, this was different. I felt it. Deep in my core. It was the same gesture, but it meant so much more. It was love. His hands were love.

"I lied to protect you." I cowardly claimed.

"I know, and you know, that that's a lie. You meant every word of it. I felt it in my spirit. I will fight with you. Fight for me. Fight for us." His voice cracked as the tears rolled down his face.

I've never seen Lee cry before. Well not since we were little, and his sister got sent away. It broke my heart into a thousand sliver pieces. Fading with the wind.

He leaned in to kiss me, but I pulled away. I must keep pretending if I am to be leader.

Giving false illusions of love will not help either of us. I love him enough to let him go. Even if my heart wants to kiss him slowly for one last time.

The shocked look on his face hurt me more than it hurt him. The matters of the heart doesn't matter at all. I will pretend as long as I have to. To protect him. From me.

"I see. Well then. I am to leave you alone at once." He bowed before me. "My future leader." It cut deeper than my daggers. Seeing him walk away. Those words broke my heart more than what it already was. Now it is I, on my knees.

"Staceyyyy." I called upon her spirits. "Why did you leave me. I need you. I need you. I." Words no longer forming as my breathes betrayed me. I felt like my windpipe was broken. Gasping. The wind suddenly made a strong appearance. Meanwhile the air was as dry as the hottest day of summer. In my heart of all hearts, I knew she was with me. I just knew.

"Stacey, I don't know what to do. Everything is bad. So bad, and I don't know if I can do this without you. I'm sorry I failed you. I failed Lee. I failed The Mother. I failed me. I'm sorry. I'm sorry. I'm sorry." My chest tightened as I dropped my head to the ground sobbing into my hands.

A firm hand appeared on my shoulder. I couldn't bare myself to look. I didn't even care. I knew it was the touch of someone trying to console me. I can tell by the way it rested softly, gripping slightly as if to massage.

When I finally breathed in deep and looked up, I felt the person's hand lift from my shoulder. I assumed it to be Thomas or father. Only no one was there. I'd been out there alone. So, who was touching me.

****

Night fell faster than any other night before it. I gulped hard in my throat. The wind is misty. Rain clearly having no mercy on me. It's also dark. Another disadvantage.

No one has ever had to endure the darkness for challenge. It was next to a death sentence.

However, tonight was the deadline. Parliament asked for an extension. Pleading that we were attacked just days ago.

We were shown no mercy. My hands were already slick of my own wetness arousing from within. I breathed in heavy. Eyes closed.

Even though I was already blind folded. I still felt a difference between the two. Idrowned out all the sounds that eroded my brain.

I'm thinking of no one. It's probably the most peace I felt in a while. I would only go when my own spirit told me so.

I kept my eyes closed. Drowning out every face I remembered before I closed them. In this moment, I realized I'm doing this because I want to.

My heart felt funny. It thundered in my chest. Riding me of all my nerves. I felt like I was in a trance. Some sort of deep REM.

The wind blew softly against my face. There goes my spirit. Telling me it's time. I screamed as I took off.

Running as if there were no ground beneath me. Never opening my eyes. I ran, and ran, and ran, and ran. I felt myself closing in as my heart continued to thunder.

I scooped up the bow and arrow and held it back for seconds before I released it. Igniting its flame, aiming it from above my shoulders. Letting it fly as I screamed again.

Eyes still closed. I felt it in my entire being. I did it. I knew it before I broke out my trance and crept back into reality.

Hearing Villagers scream in excitement. I stood there, panting. Full. I could feel the blazes of the Village symbol lit up in the sky before I could even see it. It kissed my skin like the warmth of a heated blanket draped over my shoulders in the cold of night.

Four faces making into the shape of a heart. The face of an ox, a lion, an eagle and a man. A man who in our ancient history, was the first ever leader of Blue. Who died protecting its people with the armor of his own body.

I felt bodies crowded over me. It was the first time I took the blindfold off. Standing there.

My eyes were met with the most beautiful symbolic revelation I'd ever seen. Sitting high in the sky. It is me, and I, it.

Before I knew it, I was swept up off my feet. Being paraded and carried high by many Villagers.

I saw Lee smiling from one corner. Thomas smiling from another corner, and T-B-N, bowing, standing next to The Mother and father.

For the first time, I seen acceptance spread across her face. For me. She smiled the biggest smile. Clapping her hands together. Soon, everyone followed. As they sang our creed.

        We are born again,

 born again.

        Our bright light pass

 us through

        We are born again,

 born again

        Rising into two

We scrap them from our shoe

                While we watch it from

a view

                Our Village remains

true

                Turning into

something new

                We are born again,

born again

                Our proudest,

deepest Blue

The chants faded when they set me down. My eyes landed on Lee. He held my gaze. He was proud of me. I felt it. Through all the hurt I've caused him. He was still proud of me. It only made me hurt more. He was too good a person. I didn't deserve him.

Everyone gathered around as The Mother prepared for speech.

"Tonight, is the night of a new revelation. Tonight, is a night of pain and love. We fight together, we lose together, we win together, and so we stand."

Villagers shouted in enthrallment as her gaze spoke to their souls. "The act of fate is upon us. But the battle will never be over. The day of reckoning will come, and we will have to face vexatious truths. We are favored, and they fear us. They want to take our happiness, dispose of our lives." I watched as Villagers anger grew in their chests.

They huffed and puffed. Their eyes scowled. "My daughter." She put her hand out before her, so that I, in return, will take hers. And so, I did.

"My daughter. The new leader of Blue. Will lead us to a greater salvation than anyone could ever imagine. She will guide us all. She is more chosen than any chosen. Follow her, and she will be the light in the dark. There will be a ceremony held tomorrow at dawn. Sleep well. Until tomorrow."

People slowly retreated to their homes. I basked in their smiling faces. The scent of hope lingered in the air. Swirling with the wind.

The mother and father the happiest I ever saw them. My heart beat a normal rhythm for the first time since before I ran away. I'm no fool in thinking it was over.

Thinking we all could just go back to our normal daily lives.

We're far from over. For now, I will enjoy the temporary happiness. For I know it shan't last too long.

****

Thomas was there, just as I expected him to be. Waiting for me in the commons. Snatching me from the crowd as soon as he was able to.

He took my hand in his as we slipped away to whatever secluded corner we could find.

The moment he took my hand, I felt a rush of electricity powering through my body.

It was the weirdest thing. It didn't hurt, it felt good. I even thought I caught a glimpse of light under my skin. I wondered if my powers were trying to come to me. What it even meant if those were my powers.

"You were amazing." He said pulling me into him. I was reluctant, but how could I not receive him after all he's done for me.

My guilt triggered as I thought of Lee. I'm more confused than I have ever been. Yet I remained in his space. Letting him slip his hands around my waist.

"I like to think you had something to do with it." I winked.

"No, no. It was all you."

I smiled. Thomas has a way of being coy. The most modest man I've ever met. "Oh, come on now, you deserve some credit." He released his grip on my waist. I immediately stepped away and rested my back against the wall next to him.

"I know that you have a lot going on here. I won't stand in your way. I just wanted to let you know how proud of you I am."

My fear settled in my nerves. "What are you saying. Thomas, are you leaving?" I pushed off the wall to face him.

"I am……. you are safe now. You do not need me anymore. And if ever you do, you know where to find me."

"Please reconsider. I can give you title here in Court. I am leader now you know."

He smiled. Staring into my eyes like he was searching for the pit of my soul. "You know I can't do that. I have to go back to my life. Back to my normal. This here. This is your life. It is not the way I live."

I sighed in defeat. "I know it's much to ask of you. To trade your life for me. To give up all you've ever known. But I am asking you anyway. I want you here. I need you." He moved in close on me. Dominantly towering his body over mines. "In which way do you want me." He whispered in my ear. "As what, a server, a guard……..or your mate. Because I'm telling you now. There is no way I could stay here and be able to restrain myself from kissing you." I began panting at his words. At his lips on my ears. Electricity sparking under my skin again. I longed for his touch. I longed for the promises I made Lee more.

The Black Knight appeared, and I jumped hard. Moving steps away as if I had been caught doing something wrong.

"Sorry to interrupt, you are needed at your mother's request. I was asked to escort you."

Thomas and I looked to each other. "You know where to find me." He planted a kiss to my head. I grabbed his hand and watched as it slowly disappeared. The Black Knight stood there watching it all with his face turned up. In a smirky way that annoyed me.

I didn't want Thomas to leave, but I couldn't make him stay without a promise. I'm tired of making promises I cannot keep. Walking next to T-B-N sent me an eerie feeling. A premonition attached to my gut. I hate being around him. Even if it is just a simple walk.

"You amaze me." He spoke. Straight faced as we walked. He never even looked at me. It was like he was a talking moving statue.

"Hmm." Was all I said. I refused to give a reason to further engage in any conversation with this man.

He said nothing more. When we reached the Dutch house. The Mother was eating an apple with a knife. Sitting so graciously as she always did. She was alone.

When I arrived TBN pulled out my chair for me to sit. Before he walked away, he leaned in to whisper in my ear. "You owe me a date." I jumped hard and turned to him. "I owe you nothing."

"But you do. I won the jousting. You accepted my rose and invitation. You owe me a date. Be ready tomorrow after your ceremony."

"I...I.." I stuttered angrily annoyed searching for the right words. He was already walking away.

The Mother chuckled. "He's right you know." She said continuing to eat her apple.

"Mother please don't start. It's been a long day."

"Oh dear, I know. That doesn't make him any less right."

Bothering to respond would be pointless. So, I said nothing further about it. If I am to wed him. Best I get to know him. Mother passed me an apple she sliced.

The sweet taste lingered in my mouth. Juices burst. For some reason. Flavor was more than flavor. My senses heightened a million times plus.

"I called you here to speak with you about the future. First and foremost, congratulations. I always knew you could do it."

"Thank you, Mother."

"My powers are already gone. The moment you succeeded. Which tells me yours are already in place. Have you noticed anything different?"

I sighed, slouching my body into the chair. "Not really. I thought I saw light in my body. But nothing more."

"Light." She halted everything she was doing. "That's interesting. It will take a week to fully kick in. So whatever light you saw could mean may things. We won't fully know. Let it come to you. Embrace it."

"How do I do that?"

"You simply take a deep breath, don't be afraid. Let it soak into you like second nature. You will know when the time is right."

I shook my head up and down.

"There are many things you will need to learn. I have a few advisors that will help you along the way. You can keep them on as your own or take new ones to aide you. The choice will be yours to make."

We sat in silence. Eating apples. It felt so good being with my mother. Her not shooing me away. Her proud of me. Her not making any smart remarks.

This is the moments I longed for. Soon broken by the tyranny of her next words. "Katianna, you will marry. Whether you choose it to be Sir James, Lee, the man from the woods. Whomever."

I gulped hard in my throat. Realizing for the first time that The Black Knights name was James.

"My only hope daughter is that you choose correctly for your Village, not for your own selfish heart. You must think about that when choosing. Give James a chance. It's all I ask."

"I will." I closed my eyes. "Mother are you sick?" She looked to me like there was no way I should have known that.

"I haven't been feeling well lately. We're not sure how bad it is. It could just be a common cold. David sent for special doctors. They arrive in three days. It's nothing to worry about. You just go get some rest and prepare for tomorrow."

SIXTEEN

LEE

Practice aiming is said to be one of the best forms of stress relievers. So here I am. Shooting arrows from my bow at a red target on a made-up wooden stick panel.

"Whose face are you imaging." Her voice swept my ears. Sending an immediate pulse to places where pulses don't even exist. I hate what she can do to me. The power she has. I want to hate her. Yet all I feel is her pain. I know things are not easy for her. Every decision she makes, every corner she turns, has a battle waiting for her at the end of it.

"I can actually think of a few faces." I raised my arm again to shoot. Never even glancing her direction. The tension standing between us is so thick I imagine not even the sharpest weapon could cut through.

"Would mines be one of them." She rested her hand on my shoulder.

"I rather not give away my secrets. You never know when it will be used against you." I regretted those words the moment I let them slip off my lips. Last thing I want is to be mean to her.

"Ouch." Was all she said in return. She stepped back a few feet. But she never walked away.

Even when my silence was clear. Me ignoring her and pretending like I don't want nothing more than to hold her in my arms. She still stayed. She just stood there watching me. Her lips are pinker. Her skin glowed lighter. The sweet smell of her is making it so damn hard.

"Congratulations by the way. Leader of Blue. I've always known you could do the impossible. I knew you were different." She gasped at my words. She remained silent. Until she didn't.

"Lee." She called to me as if she wasn't already near me. But I knew what she wanted. She wanted me to tell her that it was ok. Wanted me to tell her that I understood.

She wanted me to give her reassurance so that she'd feel better about it. I should give that to her so that she can go on without the mercy of worrying about me.

"Lee. Can we talk." I froze still. "Please." She added. I put the bow down and finally looked at her. My heart melted into liquid when I gazed in her eyes. It's why I hate looking at her. Always feeling like I was cast under some spell.

We began walking in no particular destination.

"Lee, I know this is difficult for you, as it is for me."

"You have no clue." I cut her off.

"I have every clue. I feel what you feel. I hurt like you hurt. It sucks for me too."

"It's not the same….and if you want me to tell you it's ok. Don't bother. Because I will never say those word, and it will never be ok."

"I'm sorry." She pulled my arm stopping us in place. "I'm so-so sorry Lee. I'm sorry for making promises I could not keep. I'm sorry you're hurting. I'm sorry."

I'm sick to my stomach with how much I want to play the victim role. I'm sick to my stomach with how badly I want to taste her. I'm disgusted with myself. I should have more control.

"Katianna, you have no idea what I am feeling. This is the hardest shit I've ever had to deal with. To lose the woman I love. To not have you. To watch you fall for another and marry another besides that…..It makes me physically sick."

"Lee, you will never lose me. I am right here. I admit when I ran off into the woods. You were all I thought about. Then I met Thomas. I grew fond of him."

My breathing grew heavy and angry at the sound of her words. I released a breath like a dragon spitting fire.

"Let me finish please." I swallowed my pride. "I met Thomas and things just happened so fast, but I never, ever, forget what I feel for you. It was stronger."

I laughed a sarcastic laugh. "Was." It was all I heard out of everything she said. Was meant past tense. No longer.

"It doesn't matter Lee. Because who I feel for means nothing. I can never be your or his. I am to be wed to a man that scares me. A man I know nothing about. A man who I don't want. He's not you."

My heart skipped in my chest. Just thinking maybe there was hope. Maybe she like Thomas, but she loves me, and hated The Black Knight.

"It matters princess….." My voice cracked. "Nothing else matters to me but that. Can't you see. Even if I was stupid enough to believe we had a shot. At least knowing you feel what I feel would mean more than not having you at all." A tear fell from her face. Her tears flowed heavier. Only they were vanished quickly. Without her even wiping at them.

"I'm…..I'm sorry Lee. You must believe me." Her sad eyes found mines. She knows I can't stand to see her cry.

"Come here." I grabbed her in my arms. "If it means that much to you. I will forgive you, but I need time apart from you. We won't be the same as we were. My heart won't allow me to be just friends."

Heat rose between us as I held her in my arms. She said no words. She just stayed in my arms like there was no other place she'd rather be.

My heart thumped faster and faster. I could feel hers too. I should be pulling away from her. Yet all I could do is stay in the moment. A moment that I'm certain will break me.

"I never meant for none of this to happen. She spoke softly.

"I know you didn't princess." I sighed. Hugging her tighter into my arms. "It's going to be ok. I have all faith in you as a leader. I will never be happy not being yours, but I will always be happy so as long as your happy."

She pushed up off my chest to look up and face me and spoke. "You will always be the one." She lingered. The way she did when I brought her a piece of bread to her chambers. I may regret it, but I took her mouth. She kissed me back. Our tongues got lost in one another's.

My heart fluttered like it was going to burst. The soft moans she let out in my mouth made me want to make love to her until the sun rose. "In case there was ever any doubt. Make no mistake. I feel what you feel." She whispered to me.

Watching her walk off was the greatest feeling. However, I'm more confused than ever. I asked for space, but she kissed me back. We both know we could never be together, yet we can't stay away from one another. This damn girl drives me insane.

The walk back to my chambers was quite interesting. I smiled to myself a few times thinking about the kiss. I strategized what I could possibly do to win her.

My imagination quickly fading at the sight of a mangy man leaning against my door. I immediately drew sword.

The man pulled down the hooded fur off his head. Revealing his identity. It was the asshole. The Black Knight.

"Sword down my boy. This is a friendly visit."

Anger grew inside me as I swiped my sword at him. He jumped back.

"Now killing or wounding a man who is unarmored is immediate grounds for death."

"What do you want." I spit at the ground where he stood.

"I just wanted to give you a message." He smirked. "She will be mines. She will fall in love with me right before your eyes. No matter how many kisses or touches you steal, she will be my wife. If I find that you ever kiss or touch her once she is wed to me. I promise you, your head will be on a pike, on display for all to see." I swiped my sword once more. "Don't worry. I'll let you watch the consummation."

Before my sword could lay wedged in his chest, guards came from all corners, holding me back as I watched him disappear from sight. I hate that pompous bastard. I can't stand him speaking of her that way.

The day I watch all the blood drain from his body, will be the happiest day of my life. For now, I will pretend. For now, her kiss is enough.

There's no way I'm going to let her be with him. Even if she can't be with me. It won't be him. There's something about that fucker. His intentions seem to be tainted.

Moments later. There was a knock at my door. I immediately drew weapon. I waited for the knock to stop. It picked up even more.

Stronger, harder, longer. I could see the knob on the door trying to turn itself. If not for me locking it after my encounter with the pompous bastard. It will have been unlocked like I normally leave it.

These days it's less likely for anyone to leave their door unlocked. Too many monsters lingering right here within these walls.

Not just the tales of the woods. The knocking proceeded. "I know you're in there. Open the door."

I sighed in relief when I heard Joes voice. What the hell could her father want now. I reluctantly opened the door.

Not knowing what was waiting for me on the other side. My trust in people is rather slim to none these days. He was alone. That eased my tension just a bit.

I opened my door all the way allowing him inside. "To what do I owe the pleasure of your presence sir." He made himself comfortable taking a seat on the chair I keep facing the window. It was my favorite spot of all. The view from my room was the most beautiful. Especially at night.

His back turned to me gave me reassurance that he came in peace. No man would ever turn their back to another. Unless they trusted.

"Marvelous view." He turned his head to acknowledge me.

"Why yes." I joined him. Standing at his side gazing out the window.

"I came to you with a proposition."

"And what might that be."

"David. The one Mary-Ann keeps so close."

"Her advisor?"

"I suppose so." He tilted his head watching as a bird flew. "I don't trust him. There is something about him that doesn't sit well with me. Follow him. Find out what's he's been up to. Find out where he goes in the middle of the night. Report back to me."

"A fool's errand. Why would I want to do that. Why have you come to me. I'm no spy. There are plenty others who are more capable than I, that can complete this request."

"Why of course. But you're in love with my daughter, they are not. You are undetected. He would not suspect a thing if you were to get caught. He knows my men."

"Again sir, with all due respect. What does that have to do with me."

"If you do this for me……help me save the woman I love. I will help you spend your life with the woman you love."

My ears dropped. "What do you mean. What saving does Mary-Ann need. How can you help me be with Katianna."

"The issues of my wife do not concern you. If you do this and bring me valuable information. I will talk with Parliament. They have powerful connections. Connections that can overrule any law. Especially one that forces marriage upon leaders."

My mouth dropped. I couldn't believe what I was hearing. There was nothing I wouldn't do. Nothing I wouldn't give to win Katianna. Even if it meant selling my soul to the devil. "Deal." I quickly responded.

"I knew you'd make the right choice." Joe stood up and shook my hand. Before walking out completely he said. "I always liked you, Lee. I know you love my daughter like no other. You are best for her."

Those words stayed with me the entire night. All this time I thought her parents hated me. I knew for sure her mother did.

To have her father blessing meant more to me than anything. It gave me a new sense of purpose. A new form of motivation. To know there was a chance. A possibility of us being together.

I had no clue what exactly he was searching for or what David did, but I did not care. I'd move the mountains off the earth if it meant I get to be with her. My only thoughts are to devise a plan. Record everything, I see. Follow him for however long.

Until I find answers. It won't be an easy task. Taking trips into the woods, or wherever he goes in the middle of the night, can be dangerous. It's a risk I'm willing to take.

SEVENTEEN

KATIANNA

"You look different."

"I feel different." I stood in the mirror with Victoria. My first chosen lady maiden. She'd always been nice to me and Stacey. It was a no brainer. Of course, I'll choose others in time. Right now, I can barely get over my heartbreak of losing my best friend. I wouldn't be able to handle too many happy ladies around me.

"You're beautiful." She expressed.

"Your too kind. Thank You." I graciously accepted.

Victoria is quiet. A blonde curly haired petite girl. So pretty and delicate like a flower.

"Are you nervous for your ceremony tonight." She asked.

"I am a bit nervous actually. I'm afraid not everyone will accept me. I know there are some who thinks I'm not ready. Some say I appear to be unstable."

"Forget them. Their stupid. If anyone is ready and capable. It is you." She brushed my hair. I closed my eyes enjoying every stroke.

"Your hair is beautiful. It's so long and silky."

"Victoria keep this up and I may have to marry you." We both giggled like little girls.

A knock at the door interrupted our laughter. Victoria opened the door. There was a guard with an envelope in his hand. "For leader Katianna." He placed the envelope in Victoria's hand. She inspected it with suspension before handing it to me.

"Whose it from?" I inspected its entirety.

"He didn't say. Open it."

I grabbed a quill off my desk and used it to glide across the top fold where the envelope sealed. In it, a note. *Make a wish it read.*

There was a dandelion flower attached to the back of the note. I couldn't help but smile ear to ear.

There was only one person this could be. Lee. He used to bring me dandelions from the fields outside all the time when we were kids, and we'd wish all our wishes. Watching each feathery bristle float away in the air. It seemed like magic to a bunch of children.

It was my favorite thing to do as a child. It was a small sentimental gesture. But a great one, nonetheless.

"What's it say." Victoria asked looking strangely upon the note and the flower.

"Nothing." I quickly countered. "Just a note mother sent me."

She raised her eyes in speculation, but she questioned me no further.

She continued to brush my hair as if nothing happened. She must have asked me a bunch of questions in between, but all I could think about was the content of that envelope, and all I want is to see him again.

****

Alone now. A rush of wind swept across the floor in my room. Sweeping past my feet.

The strangest sensation. I felt prickles under my feet as if I was being tingled by a thousand tiny needles. I felt no pain. It's like when you sit for too long and your feet goes numb.

Only I had just sat down, and the windows were shut. Leaving no explanation for the gust of wind. I closed my eyes. Remembering what Mother told me about embracing my powers.

I have this feeling that all these strange things that keeps happening to me has something to do with my powers trying to channel.

My body began to feel hot. I left my eyes closed. The deeper I sank into my thoughts the hotter my body got. It was as if I were on fire. I breathed in deep. I exhaled deeper.

The sensation tickled my insides. Suddenly it was replaced by coldness. My body got so cold. My skin felt like ice. That didn't hurt either.

The whole thing is confusing. I can't for the life of me figure out which gift were trying to come to me. Maybe it goes by how well I accept one over another.

The coldness lifted from my body, and I began to see visions. Like a daydream in real time. I saw me, Stacey, and Lee as children running around in the fields chasing each other.

My visions turned to Stacey dressed in a light blue gown. It was so light, it almost looked white. The softest blue I'd ever seen.

She was running playfully. Kind of backwards, with her hand held out, as if I was supposed to take her hand from my realm of life.

Only every time I tried to take her, she would run further and further. All she did was smile at me. She was so happy.

My heart fluttered faster as I felt the desperate need to get to her. She faded into a field of flowers. My vision took me to a war.

I stood in the middle of the most brutal battle of all time. I was mounted on a horse. Watching countless men get slaughtered. I could not tell who was who.

When a Viking man came running towards me. I jumped out the daydream.

Coming back to reality my palms were sweating. My heart was beating way past its normal rate. I was panting as if I was out of breath from running.

I don't know what it all meant. But all of it felt like Déjà vu. Only I haven't lived either of those moments, except the one of us as kids. They all equally felt so real. A knock at the door stubbed my thoughts. "Come in."

"Are you ok. You look all sweaty. You look like you've seen a ghost." Victoria spoke, returning with tea and the jewels she was sent to retrieve from my Mother.

Mother wanted me to wear her mother's pearl necklace tonight. She always told me it was a sacred piece of jewelry.

Said that it was once blessed by The Vatican itself. I for one, think it's not so appealing.

Some of its beads were scrapped. The whole necklace itself looked like it was hanging on by a thread.

However, to make her happy, to see that smile once more, I will wear it.

EIGHTEEN
KATIANNA

The ceremony is simple. The Mother and I are to face each other holding hands. The priest will pray over us both and I am to be asked if I accept my new role. I am to swear by oath.

At that time, Mother is to turn over a sealed pin with the four faces over to me.

She is to give speech first, then I to follow. Other than that, it is nothing more than a regular party. Dancing, food, wine.

The saddest part is to not have Stacey by my side. For her to see me now. I know she'd be so proud of me. Or to even have Thomas here would mean so much to me. My heart pulls for him too.

The only thing I'm not looking forward to is going on a date tonight with T-B-N. James.

"Are you ready?" Victoria asked as we looked in the mirror for final touches.

"I am ready." A blush spread across my face as I reminisced the time, I felt pleasure at the hands of Thomas.

I have no clue what's wrong with me. What I do know is that as soon as I'm able to sneak away. I will go back into the woods for him. If I could just, try to convince him again.

"You're smiling awfully a lot these days. Do tell."

"Oh nothing." I blushed harder.

"Katianna. You can trust me you know. I know I am not your best friend. I could never replace her, but you have a friend in me, and I will always be loyal to you." She said so heartfully. I believed her. I know she's a good person. I missed having girl talk with a girl. So, I opened.

"Have you ever been in love?" I asked. We both sat down on the longue facing each other.

"No, my lady. I can't say that I have. I've never even been kissed before." Her face grew sad.

"Augh, I'm so sorry. I didn't mean to…."

"It's ok. It's not your fault. I am hopeful that one day I will meet a man who will make my heart smile the way I see yours."

"And so, you shall. I have no doubt. You are beautiful."

"Thank you. Now spill…..are you in love with someone?"

My heart sank into my chest at that question. "My heart is happy and sad." The look of confusion spread on her face like wildfire. "My heart pulls for two different men. I feel like my life changed so quickly. I didn't have to time to grow up. Like I became an adult overnight, and suddenly I have all these decisions to make." She sympathized with me. Placing her hand on mine. "I don't know, I just. I just feel like I needed more time. And now I can't bear to pick one over the other. Mother wants me to marry a man I don't even know. So, my heart pulls for two, but there are three that pulls for me."

My body thundered like an earthquake was brewing inside of me. Another sign of a power perhaps.

"I'm sorry you feel this way. It mustn't be easy. But you are so strong. The prettiest girl in the village." My eyes popped at the mentioning of Victoria saying this. It was the same thing Stacey always said to me. Then she asked me. "Have you ever kissed either of them." A blush spread across my face once more.

"I've kissed them both." She squeezed my hand. Immediately apologizing afterwards. I don't blame her. I know how shocking it must sound.

"Parton me if I'm being too nosy, but who'd you feel a more meaningful kiss with. Whichever the answer to that, is maybe the right one for you."

I leaned in to hug her. It felt so good spilling my secrets to somebody. Keeping them bottled up made me want to scream from the mountains.

"That's the thing." I stood up. "I felt it deep with the both of them." I sighed. "I'm ready." I spoke. Victoria walked to the doors letting the guards in to escort me downstairs.

"Victoria." I called to her before leaving.

"Yes, my lady."

"Do you live in the Dutch House, or do you live in Cottage?"

"Cottage." She smiled.

"Will you consider moving in Dutch House? I will have a chamber made for you."

She bowed gracefully. "Thank you, my lady. That is so generous. Can I think about it? It's just that I have younger siblings I look after."

"Of course. If you accept, they can come too." I winked at her before leaving.

****

The decoration display was a little gaudy. Not exactly my taste. But if I know Mother, there was no way this ceremony would be anything other than.

My heart galloped as we stood facing each other. Hundreds of people flooded the hall.

Standing here holding her hands. I felt an electric shock. One that caught her attention as if she felt it too. We starred deeper into each other eyes.

When the priest finish blessing and praying, Mother handed over the sacred pin of the four faces. She pinned it to the left side of my dress. Near my heart.

"Do you solemnly swear to be the keeper of Blue. To protect the Village and its people until the day you die.?"
"I do."

"Do you swear to obtain a husband within thirty days.?" I gulped hard in my dry throat. "I do."

"And do you swear to make decisions to the best of your ability on behalf of Blue. To treat everyone fair and kindly and punish those who are at fault.?"
"I do."

"Then I pronounce you the new leader of Blue. Katianna Mary-Ann Hansely. Long may you reign."

Mother smiled. I smiled. Everyone cheered. She hugged me tight. "You're special." She whispered in my ear.

Father came up first to congratulate me. A slew of people followed. I must have given hugs to hundreds. My arms were sore.

"Dance with me?" T-B-N offered. Extending his hand to mine.

"I'll pass."

"You want me to beg do you." He got on one knee. "Will. You. Please. Dance.With.Me" He shouted into the crowd. Causing attention our direction.

"Get up. You're making a fool of yourself."

"I don't mind being a fool for you." His eye glared. I hate the way he looks at me.

"Fine, just get up."

He got up taking my hand in his. Leading me to the dancefloor. He bowed before wisping me into his arms.

A tingle rushed down my spine. He swayed us all around. I wanted it to be awkward. I wanted to appear to be uncomfortable.

Only I wasn't. One thing I give him, is that he was the best dancer I knew. "You are more beautiful than the stars in the sky, and stars are my favorite thing to look at." A small smile crossed my face. "Is that a smile." He noticed. "No." I quickly countered.

"Congratulations by the way."

"Thank You."

"I can't wait till this evening is over. I'm excited for our date."

"Why? Why are you trying so hard. What's your end game?"

"You." He wisped me off my feet and spun me around in the air, catching me perfectly. "My end game is you." He whispered staring into my eyes.

The song stopped, and we stayed there in each other's arms. Staring. Someone coughed in the crowd bringing us back to reality.

I hope he didn't think I was staring with the same admiration as him. I was staring searching for answers in his eyes.

I have a good way of reading people through their eyes. It tells me all I need to know.

All his eyes were telling me was that he meant what he said. Either he's a master manipulating con artist, or he likes me.

"Meet one hour after the party. Will you light a candle in your window to let me know when you're ready?"

I reluctantly shook my head yes. "I'll be looking for that light. Light two. I have to make sure I know it's the candle and not you. You shine brighter."

A small spread across my face again. Against my will. I can't stand him. He's good at what he does.

"Dance with me." I grabbed Victoria's hands. She willingly followed. We danced forever. It reminded me of Stacey. I have no idea why she reminds me so much of her, but she does.

"This is fun. I really hope you consider my proposal." I told her. She looked confused. "What proposal." She asked. Now, it is I who looked confused. "The one I asked you just moments before the party started silly. Did you forget already?"

A look of complete oblivion spread on her face. "What are you talking about my lady. I haven't seen you all day." I stopped dancing. I was confused.

How could she say this. How could she not remember. She brushed my hair. I told her secrets, and now she's pretending to not know what I'm talking about. My head started spinning.
I began to feel lightheaded.

"Are you ok my lady." She asked.

"I'm fine. I must go." I was losing my mind. Maybe it was my powers hallucinating.

Maybe she was never there. I walked off in the direction of my chambers.

The Mother shouting to me as I passed to not forget tomorrows first meeting. I gave her a nod and continued walking.

I needed a drink of water. I needed to lie down for a few minutes. I wish my powers would make up its mind, because it's messing with my head.

When I cut through the back of the kitchen to get to my chambers faster. Lee was there sipping wine and eating cheese and apples.

With some women I don't know. Immediate rage boiled inside me. I felt my body getting hot as it did earlier.

My eyes flashed red as I could see it in the reflection from the kitchen mirror.

"Congratulations." Lee moved away from the girl towards me with his arms open. I quickly pushed his arms down.

"What's wrong." His face surprised at my reaction. The girl stood by looking immensely at us both. "Your hands are hot." He said looking down at his arms where I left a mark.

"Don't you dare…. don't touch me…don't ask me what's wrong. I was just converted and you're in the back of the kitchen with some whore having fine wine and cheese." My chest heaved up and down as I grew angrier.

My skin was burning from the inside. "He kissed me just yesterday you know." I spat a look of fire in her direction. She smiled smirky as my comment had no effect.

"Your coronation was beautiful. I watched every bit of it. When James took your hand to dance, I left to the kitchen to find comfort in a bottle of wine. My sister Allison here." He pointed at the girl "Came all the way from the other side of the world, to witness your coronation. She traveled two days to get here. When she saw I was upset, she followed me into the kitchen."

The air wrapped its grip around my body in embarrassment. I hadn't seen Allison since she was a little girl.

She was two years younger than us. She always trailed behind us. Always running to catch up, the way I did with Mother when I was her age.

She was sent away ten years ago. Certainly not the little girl I remembered.

She stood tall and slim. Body full to its growth. Her hair was blonde like her brothers. Blue eyes. She was this beautiful at seventeen.

I can imagine what else is to become of her. The heat in my body faded as I took several calming breaths.

"Still pretending like you don't like my brother, but still get mad at the thought of him with another." Allison spoke. Smiling ear to ear. Her accent was so strong and thick. She was definitely a Dane, and her Danish accent is sexy.

I ran to her taking her in my arms. She embraced with just as much enthusiasm. "My apologies. I am so so sorry Allison. I thought..I."

"No need for apologies. I know what you thought. I've missed you."

"I've missed you too. My have you grown. You're gorgeous."

"As are you sister." I smiled at that. She used to call me sister when we were kids. She could never pronounce my name.

"What made you come here after all these years."

She sighed leaning back on the table. "I've always wanted to come back, but mother always told me she'd send for me when the time was right. When I got word of your coronation. I demanded to come home. I told them I would refuse to eat or follow any rules." We all laughed. "They allowed me a week's clemency."

"Well, I am so glad you're here. I cannot wait to catch up. I have a first duty meeting tomorrow. Can we do lunch after?"

"Of course, she said, wrapping her arms around me this time. "I'll let you two talk. Brother you know where to find me." She winked at Lee as she walked off. Leaving us awkwardly alone.

We both leaned against the table.

"I'm s….." We both began to speak at the same time. "You first." He insisted.

I swallowed my pride. "I'm sorry for getting angry. Seeing you with….. well, the thought of you with another channeled an anger in me I could not control. I know it isn't fair, but I can't help how I feel Lee." My eyes gazed to his.

He took my hand. "You never have to apologize for your feelings. I will never be with another women. It is you I want." He blinked his eyes. "I've been a jealous fool. I know that. I asked for time, I know that, but you are on my mind constantly. It drives me mad. You. Drive. Me. Mad."

His fingertips trailed up and down my arms. I closed my eyes to his touch. Remembering the day in the woods.

What the fuck is wrong with me. Get some control now.

He pushed himself from the table, facing me now. Standing right in front of me. I opened my legs.

Gesturing him to stand in between my thighs. All different kinds of senses pinged off inside of me. Electric, heat, lust.

He walked in between my legs. Gripping his hands at my waist. "Do you remember what I told you that day we almost lost control." I swallowed my spit.

"I remember." I said shakily. My voice creaked and cracked. He kissed my shoulder.

The warmth of his lips pressed against my skin made me tingle and wet between my thighs. "You're making it so dam hard." He kissed my neck, using tongue.

"Because all I want is to lift this pretty dress of yours. Right here on this table and taste all the juices that I know is dripping between your legs." He glided his hand up my dress until he found my panties.

He pushed them aside and slid his fingers on my wet clit. Rubbing up and down. I gasped as I threw my head back. Soft moaning in his ears. He kissed me. I kissed him back. "Your so fucking pretty princess. I'm going to make my little princess cum all over my fingers." He sucked on my neck while continuing to rub his fingers up and down my clit.

I panted heavy, grinding myself back and forth on his fingers, until my pussy clinched in his hands. He covered my mouth with the hand that was once around my waist.

As he continued to rub my clit even while I was coming. He sucked on my neck until I stopped screaming.

A tear fell from my eye. I felt my climax so deeply. Deeper than I ever have before.

It was as if I was one with the earth, and my orgasm was more than my own pleasure.

He took his hands from underneath my dress and slid his fingers in his mouth. Looking at me while I watched him suck every bit of me off his fingers.

"Mmmmm." He spoke. "The sweetest thing I ever tasted." He leaned in to whisper in my ear. "Now think about that while you're on your date."

He kissed my forehead. "Princess." He winked and walked away. Leaving me there. Vulnerable. Lusting.

Confused. Panting. *Well played Lee.*

It took minutes for me to gather myself off the table. I can't believe what just happened. Where the hell did this bad boy Lee come from. I can't say I hate it.

I ran off to my chambers and straight into the bath. I only had a few minutes before I had to be ready.

NINETEEN

KATIANNA

I lit two candles in my window. No later than a few minutes did I hear pebbles being thrown at my window.

I crept to the window and opened it. Surprised to see T-B-N standing beneath my window. Dressed so casually.

A horse and carriage waited by his side. "For you, my lady." He said shouting up to me. I've been in horse and carriage plenty of times in my travel. Never one this beautiful. Never one on a date.

We sat opposite sides. Staring at each other the whole ride as if we were in some sort of unspoken blinking contest. He said not one word.

When we came to halt. The driver dismounted from the horse, walked around to the opening, and let us out the carriage.

Stepping out the carriage I walked into the most beautiful scene. It was a picnic under the stars.

He knew exactly what spot to take us to. It was the most secluded star gazing, mountain viewing, water falling, spot I'd ever seen.

He must have had help. There were very few people in Blue who knew about this spot.

There were two big blankets covering the grass, and one big, folded blanket that rested on it. Trays of food, a wine bottle with two glasses, and paper with quills.

I was confused about the paper and quills. There were roses layed in the middle.

He took my hand and led me onto the blanket. Finally breaking our silence, I said. "Nice set up. I can imagine how many girls you trick to come here." He smirked.

"I am not blue, I am black. I've never brought a girl here before. You are the first....and hopefully the last and only."

"Hmm." I sighed.

"Wine?" he asked as he reached for the bottle and glasses. I reluctantly shook my head yes.

The cork popped sending my ears to pull back. He poured wine in my glass, then in his. "To new friendships." He said holding his glass up. "Cheers." I clicked my glass to his. Sipping slowly.

My nerves won't settle as I sat there tensed. "You can relax you know." His brow furrowed, but he didn't look at me.

"I am relaxed." He laughed at my response.

"You couldn't be more nervous than a scared cat in the corner."

I sighed in frustration. "I assure you, there's nothing scared about me. I don't know you. I don't trust you. I will always be guarded."

"Take a look around. There is nothing to not trust. Just breathe."

Reluctantly I sank my shoulders trying to find myself at ease.

"What's the paper and quill for?"

"It's for when you get more comfortable. When you do. I'll tell you." He layed down on his back. I layed down on my back moments after. I see what he saw. I see why he wanted to lay. The stars were beautiful. They flooded the sky like a bed of flowers in the field growing naturally.

"When I was a boy, my mother use to bring me outside at night to watch the stars with her. She'd always tell me stories about her childhood and how she met my father." He never turned to face me, he just kept watch up in the sky, at the stars. I could see the stars from the sky in his eyes. His eyes were my mirror. "What's happened to her?"

He sucked in a deep breath. Relaxing his shoulders.

"She got sick in a plague years ago. She died when I was twelve. I was raised by my father. He was nowhere near soft like my mother. He was the opposite in fact. He'd banned me from going out at night to see the stars. Said it made little boys grow up to be whimps. He'd always tell her: *I'm not raising a whimp, I'm raising a Viking.*

He was a cruel man. It wasn't until I became a grown man was I able to see the stars again. To remember her again."

I felt bad for him. His story sounds tragic. No child should ever have to go without the love of their mother. It made sense to me now. Why he is the way he is.

I sat up to sip the rest of my wine. Helping myself to another glass. If I am to get through this night. It be best I drank.

I began eating the grapes and crackers and cheese and apples, as my hunger grew. I hadn't eaten at the party. I didn't realize I was eating like a pig. "Sorry." I wiped crackers from the corner of my mouth. Realizing he was staring at me.

"It's all yours, no apology necessary." He smiled. He sat up pouring himself another glass. "Any siblings?" I asked. "Only child." He tells me.

I had hope for him. Hope that the love of a sibling wouldn't be so bad without a missing parent. I feel even worse for him now.

"I know your mother is trying to force me on you, but that is not the way I want it to be. I want you to be happy. I want you fall for me because it's what you feel in your heart, and for no reason other than that. And if it doesn't happen…." He gazed to me. "If you don't fall for me. I still wish you happiness, and I will still fight besides you. No matter what. I want you know that."

"I appreciate your kind words." Slivers of hope emerged at the pit of my heart. Maybe he's not at all what I thought he was.

I leaned my arms behind me so that I held myself up with the palms of my hands. Closed my eyes and titled my head back. I sucked in the deepest breath.

I smell the sky. The stars were kissing my eyelids. The wind sang in my ear. The crickets danced all around me. The waterfall enveloped my body.

This is the most in touch with earth I've ever felt. Upon opening my eyes, he was staring at me in complete endearment. I held his gaze. "You are stunning." I blushed at his words. "Are you going to tell me what the paper and quill is for now?"

He gathered the paper and quill in his hand. "We will both write something. On one side, write down two truths and one lie, on the other side write a letter to your younger self. After the night is over, we will exchange papers. After learning more about one another tonight, we are to write on each other's paper what we think the two truths are and what we think the lie is."

This was interesting to me. I played along in his little game. I'm kind of curious to see what his paper will say. We both got to writing.

After we finished. He folded our papers and put them into sealed envelopes with our names on it.

We spent time playing tic tac toe on the remaining papers. Which he won all three times by the way. It was so annoying.

Three drinks and a bunch of food later, I was loose. More comfortable than I would like to be around him.

"Dance with me?" He got up extending his hand to me to pull me up.

"You're crazy. There's no music." I stood. Taking him up on his offer to pull me up.

"We don't need music. We have stars." He looked up. I followed his eyes to the sky.

He took my hand and swayed me in his arms. This time, way slower than how we danced at the parties.

I rested my head on his shoulder. He slipped one hand to the small of my back. Causing me to gasp at his grip.

His touch was nice. Different from Lees and Thomas. I hated myself for even comparing them at this moment.

I swayed with him wondering how it could be possible. For every person to have such a different touch and effect.

I imagined a hand is just a hand. I closed my eyes and found myself daydreaming again. I heard music in my own head.

The soft sound of a Cello played in my eardrums. When I opened my eyes, he was looking down to my head resting on his shoulders.

He tilted my chin up with his hand. I lingered. Why did I linger. *Shit.* He leaned in towards my face and I stupidly leaned upwards to meet him halfway. His lips met mines.

He held the back of my neck shoving his tongue into my mouth. His tongue was juicy. It tasted like the wine we'd been drinking. I couldn't stop. I wanted to stop.

He picked me up in his arms, carrying me to the blanket, and I didn't stop him. *Damn wine.*

It doesn't help that I'm attracted to him and his stupid smile. His dimples were sexy. He's so muscular. I felt it when I grabbed onto his arms when he picked me up.

We continued kissing on the blanket, under the stars. He respected me, never going any further than just the kiss.

I felt the connection. I hate him for it. I'm so screwed. The last thing I needed was another person added to my bleeding heart.

We gathered our things and headed back into the carriage. I couldn't bare looking at him on the ride home.

He seemingly took pleasure at my flushed face, as he kept his eyes on me the whole time as I looked out the side made up plastic window.

When we arrived. He walked me inside and gave me the envelope with his name on it. "I had a great night." He brought my hand up to his lip. Planting a firm but soft kiss. "When you're ready, you open it. We'll exchange them back whenever you say. "Sleep well." He said.

I said goodnight as we parted ways. The moment I reached inside my chambers.

I threw my back against the door. Slowly sinking myself to the floor.

Hitting my palm against my head. "What are you doing, what are you doing." I said to myself.

****

"Have you slept at all." Mother asked pulling loose strands of hair behind my ear. "I told you to get rest after the party. What's happened to you." She looked me up and down as we were the first to arrive at Parliament.

She spit in her hands using it to glide down my hair in a desperate attempt to fix me up last minute. I shooed her hands away from me. "Mother please." She did that to me as a child. I hated it then; I hate it even more now. "I couldn't sleep last night."

She raised her eyebrows. "I can see that. Your eyes are puffy and dark. Sit up straight."

Parliament entered one by one. The meeting began. Which mainly consisted of Mr. Punic handing me over mountains of paperwork to look over. They gave me a map of our lands. I am to learn it like the back of my hand.

They gave me different options of how to proceed regarding the situation of our Village being attacked.

I had to answer to the situation with the crops, the wood, the livestock. It was all too much, too soon. If this is what Mother had to endure, I feel sorry for her.

"Give her a little time gentleman. She only was changed just yesterday." Mother spoke.

"It's either she's ready or she's not. There is no giving of the time." Mr. Punic yelled. Spit flew out of his mouth. Spit was always flying out of his big fat mouth.

"She passed challenge just recently. Everyone, including myself had weeks to prepare when we first began."

"That is her problem, not ours. Nobody told her to run away for months."

I slammed my hand to the table. Standing up. Trembles rolled over the table as I slammed it down. "Dare watch your fat tongue Punic. I am in no mood today. I will get it right, but what you will not do is disrespect me or my mother. Or you will find yourself off the board. Got it." I zeroed my eyes in on him.

He and everyone else looks shocked. Hell, I don't even know what's gotten into me. He sank into his chair, nodding his head up and down.

I let them know Victoria will be picking up all my new personal belongings (the map, paperwork, etc....) and that we will have another meeting in five days, when I am better caught up.

    No one dare questioned me. I think I could get used to this.

TWENTY

KATIANNA

A knock at my door woke me up. I looked towards my window, realizing I slept longer than I wanted, Nightfell already.

I wasn't sure what exact time it was, but I knew I missed lunch with Allison. I probably missed dinner too. I dragged myself out of bed to answer the door.

It was Victoria. She had a tray of food in her hand, confirming my thoughts about missing dinner.

"Hello sleepy head." She expressed. "Your mother told us all to let you sleep. That you are not to be disturbed." She placed the tray on the table. I grabbed the cup of water desperately as my throat thirsted for moisture. Downing it like it was the last thing I'll ever drink. "What time is it?"

"Seven p.m."

I grunted. I hate myself right now. What I must look like to people. Their new leader, partying, drinking all night, yelling in meeting, sleeping till nighttime. It doesn't look good. I promised myself that as of tomorrow I will take everything more seriously.

"Victoria…..are you ok? Yesterday you acted strangely." Her eyes popped.

"I wasn't feeling to well yesterday my lady. My apologies."

"It's ok. I'm just worried about you. Is all."

She smiled. "Everything's fine now."

"So did you think about my offer."

"I have, and umm, well…I'm sorry my lady I will have to decline. My sisters and I are quite the handful. I wish to be no burden."

"Nonsense. I insist. I can give all of your sister's title here. They will be no burden. How old are they? I have two siblings myself. Both boys. Noah and Joe jr." She smiled, but her smile still told me she was reluctant. "I don't mean to push; it's just….. I like you, Victoria."

"I'm flattered my lady. I promise I'll think on it some more. Can I give you answer in a few days?"

"Sure….of course." I assured her. Although I was confused. I was offering her a deal of a lifetime. Any lady would be honored. My suspension risen about Victoria.

She washed my back as I took a bath. I was eager to see outside my room. Allison was in the commons when I walked through. People bowed as I walked past. They didn't have to, it was no requirement of mines, like it was Mothers.

"Allison." I called to her, greeting her with a kiss on each cheek.

I sat beside her. "My apologies. I overslept."

"It's fine." She put her hand of my face. "We'll catch up now."

We must have spent hours laughing. Retelling stories of things we remembered from the past. She is truly like a little sister to me.

I was sad to see Allison leave. She'd grown on me in these five days. Like the sister I never had. She was certainly the perfect distraction. We talked a lot about the past. What I liked most about her was that she didn't question me about her brother or my personal life.

She told me Lee would send for her on her eighteenth birthday. I told her I would make sure of it. She helped me learn every name of every Villager. She created a rhyme to match each person's description. I must have studied day and night. She'd always come to my chambers and stayed as long as she could.

During the next five days I set up meetings of the land. It's when Villagers come before you with their issues, and I had to listen carefully and resolve any problems I could.

It was held each morning for two hours. Mainly consisting of stolen property, marriage proposals, sickness, fights, and all sorts of tedious problems.

Everyone was in training aside from children under the age of sixteen. I've had people come to complain about which station they were sent to train.

They complained jousting was too hard, so they'd prefer to be put on bow and arrow. I've had two siblings fighting over the same girl.

One wanted the other thrown in the black hole. The problems were endless. I never paid much attention to this part of being leader. Every time I saw Mother solving issues, it seemed so quick and easy. Now that it is I, I'm finding it rather annoying.

The meeting I promised Parliament was tonight. My five days were up. I feel much more competent than I did days ago.

Mother was no longer apart of the meetings. She was only allowed to sit in on day one. Now I must take complete responsibility.

She's taught me all she knew. I have no doubt I will be fine. Besides, she's been ill for some days now.

Special doctors came in a couple days ago to have a look at her.

They gave no explanation to her condition. They only said it must pass on its own, but to be prepared for the worst.

"Do you plan to retaliate against the Villages who almost caused us a wipe-out?" Mr. Punic spoke first. He wasted no time getting to the point.

"It is my understanding that we won that battle. As, I recall, per section twelve, article three, no retaliation is needed when the war has been won in the favoring party side. Do correct me if I am wrong."

His face twisted up in disgust as he heard me speak. I knew all too well that they want revenge. We all do. But it will be when I say, when the time is right. Not now when they most expect it.

"Next question."

"Do you plan to marry soon. You have only days left to wed. From what I know, there are no wedding plans made."

I scowled my eyes at Sir William. How dare he.

"Ask me something that doesn't concern you. My personal life is no concern of yours." Members began to chuckle under their breath. I cannot believe I'm in a room full of overgrown men and their acting like a bunch of little girls.

He cleared his throat. "Right. My apologies. There is the matter of the Black Field Festival."

"What about it."

"Well, I assume it will be no more. Seeing as how all the Villages are against one another."

"The Black Field Festival will continue each year as it always has." Everyone squirmed in their seats. "We. Are. The. Main. Source. In case anyone of you haven't noticed. They need us more than we need them. I promise, they will be begging for it. Any bad blood between the Villages will be in treaty for that one day only. They come to our territory. We will always have the upper hand. Business is Business. They won't be stupid enough to try anything."

The room stood quiet. Nobody else could think of any questions to ask.

"Gentlemen. If there is nothing else. I have other things to do." I gazed around the room. Looking for anyone who had something to say.

"What do we do about the prisoners in the black hole. Some have been down there for days. Nobody's talking."

"Use reinforcements. Threaten their titles and lands. Shed blood. Make them talk. If still no one talks. I will pay a personal visit, and that won't end well. You can tell them I said that." I rose from my chair. They rose from theirs in respect. I gave the ok for them to sit. Mr. Punic said he had one last question. "Go ahead." I nodded my headed.

"We were all wondering what powers the Gods gifted you. We've heard many stories. They say you are the chosen one. Highly gifted. Is it true."

I winked and they watched as I walked out the room. For some reason, my patience has been stretched thin these days.

Especially since I've been worried about Thomas. I received a letter saying he wanted to meet with me tomorrow afternoon. In the fields, near the willows.
It's strange.

Part of me wondered if he was in trouble, or if he just wanted to see me because he missed me.

I found it stranger that the letter asked if I could come alone.

Why would Thomas ask me to come alone. I alerted Father, Lee, T-B-N, and my guardsmen to stay hidden, but stay nearby. I told them I will give a signal to leave if there were no danger.

TWENTY-ONE

KATIANNA

The afternoon couldn't come fast enough. I rushed to the fields. Only to find that no one was there.

I remained mounted on Stella. She's my horse gifted to me from The Vatican when I was converted. Beautiful.

All black with the shiniest coat of hair. I developed a strong relationship with her instantly. She pranced around a bit as if she was nervous. "Stella girl. Relax." I rubbed her at her sides.

There goes that premonition feeling again. I looked around, almost ready to ride off when I saw Thomas appear.

It was Thomas, but he seemed different. He looked serious. My heart galloped. "Thomas is everything alright. I received your letter." He looked at me strangely.

It was like he was looking through me, not at me. I never dismounted. I knew something was off. Had he turned his back on me for some strange reason.

Stella attempted to ride off, but Thomas grabbed me at my legs causing me to fall.

I could hear my people running across the fields to get to me. I was thankful that I was smart enough to come up with the idea. Imagine if I had gone alone.

"What is your problem." I yelled to him as he pinned me down. My body beginning to hotten. "If you don't let me, go, I will hurt you." He said nothing.

He pulled a knife to my throat. I quickly froze his hand. "I don't know what's gotten into you, but you better come to your senses and quick. Once they near us. I won't be able to save you. What is wrong with you. Talk to me."

I released my freeze allowing him a chance to talk, but all he did was attack again. I froze him once more. Something moved near me.

I knew it wasn't one of my peoples because I could still see them running towards me.

The closer this thing got, the more I panicked. Before my eyes, stood the same wolf from the woods the day I was being held with a sword to my neck and it came in my defense.

The wolf lunged at Thomas, biting at his arm. Everyone arrived by now.

Grabbing Thomas from the ground. I was so hurt and confused. The wolf bit at Thomas legs. I had to freeze it in order to stop it.

Because even after what was so mind boggling about this circumstance. I knew there had to be a reason. I just knew it, and I didn't want to see him hurt.

"Take him to the hole." I ordered. More strange events occurred. Thomas wasn't Thomas at all. Thomas was Willow. Her body appeared replacing Thomas. "Shapeshifter." I yelled at her. "You're a goddam shapeshifter." She laughed in my face.

"Aww. You poor thing. You didn't think you was the only one with a power did you." We all stood around shocked at what was happening.

"Of course not. I had no idea you were even converted."

"I was converted same day as you. Only no one noticed. No one cared because everything is always all about you."

"So is that why you tried to kill me. That is treason. No matter who you are. No one leader could attempt or take another leaders life without immediate threat or probable cause. And I did no such thing to you."

"Fuck the rules. You bitch." She spat on my face. Disgusting vile. I grew angry channeling my fire.

I panted heavy until my body turned red. Flames blazed as I channeled. I wanted nothing more than to spit back on her with fire.

Turning her into dust where she stood. Thomas appeared in the fields.

The real Thomas. The wolf immediately retreated to his side. Vanishing in thin air. It was like I was the only one who saw it.

His eyes told me to breathe and calm down. Everyone stared, moving several feet away. The heat of my blaze would burn anyone near it.

It wasn't the first time they saw it. Two days ago, a Villager made me so angry I channeled my fire. Causing everything around me to burn. It was bad.

The whole west wing has to be redone because of it. The hardest thing about channeling, is learning control. It's like a newborn vampire thirsting for blood.

It's the hardest thing to constrict when it's new. My flames died down. "Take her to the hole." She looked to me.

"It's ok, because I know all your dirty little secrets, and I plan to voice them at the hearing." They grabbed her, taking her away.

I walked to Thomas. He wrapped his arms around me. For the first time ever. Lee stood next to T-B-N, and there was no battle.

They had something in common. Their hatred for Thomas. I nodded my head to tell them to give me privacy. Neither of them moved.

They looked to each other, then back to me. I gave a final warning with my eyes. They walked off in opposite directions.

"I've missed you." I wrapped my arms around him this time.

"I've missed you more."

We continued walking. "So, tell me. How is that you knew to show up. If she shapeshifted as you. Then that means she knows who you are to me, but it also means she channeled you here."

"She didn't channel me here. I channeled myself here." I stopped in place.

"But how. I mean. Wait, what." He shook his head and smiled at me.

"There's something I've been wanting to tell you." We picked back up walking. My ears were all open. "I can channel.

My power is astral projection, along with wolf. Remember the story I told you about my Village being burned down?"

"Yes. Of course, I do."

"Well. I was a line leader for that Village. Grey. Grey Village. A man once came to see me in the woods. An old man. He told me of my powers and said he knew who I was. He told me I was the chosen leader of a Village that no longer existed. He said the Gods was so powerful that even after my lands were demolished, I was still destined. Therefore, was gifted my abilities at a younger age than most. I've only channeled it three times in my life. When I was a young boy. The day I watched my family die. Only my wolf was a young. Had no strength against an army of men. It only happens when I love another. Almost like an imprint. Like a protective shield. Whenever I see or sense someone I love in danger. Only then can I channel the wolf, or astral project it."

"Is that why you hid away all your life……in the woods?" Silence split the air between us.

"Apart of the reason yes. I was too afraid to understand what it was. I was afraid I was a freak. Afraid of when it would come out again. Afraid of if I ever fell in love, I couldn't control it."

"The day we were caught. When that bastard held his sword to my neck…..was that you? I saw a wolf. The wolf helped me."

"Yes. It was me."

"Oh Thomas, I'm sad for you to have lived like this for so long. I wish you would have told me."

"I wanted to tell you. I Just…." He stopped speaking.

"You're afraid I'd know that you love me." I stopped walking. It was my honor. I had to look him in his eyes.

"Yes." He smiled. His dimples were even deeper than I remembered. "I have heightened senses that alerts me when someone I love is in danger. The moment it triggered for you. I astral projected my wolf. He's much faster than I."

This whole situation is bat shit crazy. Willow and her shapeshifting. Thomas and his secret powers. Me with my powers all in one.

"I see that you're a fire wielder." He laughed.

"Yes. That, amongst many other things."

"Many other things." He raised a brow.

"Yes. I was gifted a very powerful gift. I'm a spirit-er. I have all powers. I can project any power I want at any given time, if I channel it. Every power that each leader of a Village has. I have."

"Wow. That's amazing. Wow."

"Yup. I haven't told everyone yet. Only a few people know. So please don't go telling my secrets."

"Me." He smiled. "Never."

He grabbed me swinging me into him. Holding me like he did that day. Our last day in his Cottage.

"I channel my fire more than anything." I shook my head. "It comes when I'm mad."

"So let me get this straight. You can channel fire, wind, water, shapeshifting, astral projection, is there anything I'm missing?"

"Freezing, electricity, and earth manipulation. I can also channel spirits."

"Channel spirits. As in talk to the dead?"

"Sort of. I can connect my mind to the past or future."

He asked no more questions about it. I was happy because it was all new to me. I wasn't sure if I could fully explain myself. All I know is that I can channel any one of those powers depending on my thoughts and mood.

Thomas walked me and Stella back to the Commons. "Will you stay. Please?"

"You know I don't like when you say please. Besides it looks a bit crowded." He nodded his head towards Lee and T-B-N, who stood at the entrance of the Commons, pretending like they were both busy. Pretending like they weren't waiting for me. "Just for supper." I pouted my lips.

"Ok…ok…Just for dinner." He took off on the grounds. Seemingly as if he knew the Village. Like it was home to him. When just days ago I redirect him to where everything was.

T-B-N wasted no time beating Lee to the punch. "May I speak with you?"

"Can it wait until tonight. I'm off to visit my parents." His teeth gritted as he jerked his head in defeat. "Of course." He spoke. "Please don't forget. It's important."

"I'm sure it is. I won't forget."

TWENTY-TWO

KATIANNA

The Mother looked so peaceful sleeping in her bed. Her sickness appeared to be getting worse. She's now with fever. She moved her arms when she felt my presence. Father had already left the room. It hurts me to see him hurting. He's the best noble man I know.

Always fair, always patient, always willing to lend a listening ear. He cared so much about each and every person's induvial problem.

"Come my child. Sit." She beckoned for me patting her hand on the bed next to where she laid. Mother has never invited anyone to sit on her bed before. Only father. She smiled when she felt the weight of my body sink into the mattress. "You're so pretty my girl. Always shining brighter than the light itself. You always had a glow to you." I smiled at her.

"Do me one favor." She continued. "Raise Noah and Joe as your own. Protect your little brothers. Always think smart. Don't lead with love. It will be the death of you." Her arm went limp as she attempted to raise it. She was weak. So weak.

"Mother you speak as if you are already gone." A slight smile tried to form her lips, only those were weak too.

"Tomorrow is promised to no one dear."

"Of course not, but there's always hope."

She sighed softly. It was barely there at all. "That's one thing that distinguishes me from you. Your hope. It's so prominent to you. Whereas I...I believe hope is an excuse for unspoken defeat."

She tried to sit up, but her body flew back against her. "Mother, careful." I rushed to aid her.

I lifted her body against the headboard so that she'd have something holding her up. I fluffed her pillow and leaned her back again.

She pointed at the tea that had been sitting on the nightstand for God knows how long.

There were all kinds of debris floating atop. "I will send for you a new tea. Guards." I shouted at the doors. "Send for Victoria. Tell her I request tea." The guard nodded and went about.

"I want you to know something." She looked at me with sad eyes. "I know that I haven't been the softest, or even a loving mother. But I raised you the way I did for a reason. You see Kati, the world is harsh. There's no room in it for weak people. But know this. I love you. I love you so much. You are, and always will be my favorite. Don't tell the boys." Tears rolled down her face, as well as mines. Silent tears. We still chuckled.

Never in a million lifetimes would I have imagined she would say those words. "I'm proud of you. I have no doubt you will be the strongest and longest lasting leader Blue have ever seen, and your name.... your name will go down in history so hard that it will change the face of time. You will become a symbol. Next to the man in the torch." My tears kept rolling down my face. Uncontrollably. I felt like I was suffocating.

My breathes slowed as I sat there listening to her. For some reason I felt like it was last time I would ever see her alive. "Your powerfully gifted. A spirit-er. All in one, you are. That's amazing. Never question your powers. I once said you were more chosen than chosen, and now you know why. But Kati." She finally turned her head to face me. "Don't over or underestimate your powers. It's a gift and a curse." I had no clue what she meant by that.

I was crying too much to ask her to elaborate. It didn't matter what she meant. I interlocked our fingers together. Hand in hand. The way I did when I was a little girl.

Desperate to follow my mother everywhere she went. I could never keep up.

She was always stepping ahead of me. So, I would always grab her hands so that she couldn't go too far. Even if it meant me nearly being dragged with my feet lifted off the ground.

"Mother I love you. I've always looked up to you. I've always yearned for your acceptance. I……I" The words were no longer forming.

The waterpower's began channeling under my skin. I could feel the coldness. The more emotions I go through, the more I'm starting to realize which powers will come out.

So far, I know when I'm mad, fire, when I'm sad, water, when I'm intrigued or aroused, electric. My electric can go both ways. If my electric channels through anger, there is certainly nothing or no one safe next to me.

She said nothing more. I said nothing more. I just stayed there. I stayed until she fell asleep.

Her body was drooping over to the side and when I went to lay her down. There was a knock at the door. "Enter." It was David. He told me it was time for her medicine.

I'd ask him what he'd been giving her. He assured me it was natural remedies that aided her pain and helped her sleep peacefully. I left him to it.

As I walked out her chambers puffy eyed, and sad. To hear her tell me she loves me and she's proud of me was one of the best things that's ever happened to me.

It's all I ever wanted all my life. Even if it happened the way it's happening. With her, practically knocking on deaths door. It's still the sliver of love I needed, from her.

Upon returning to my chambers, I sat at the table. Removing everything on it with the swipe of my hand. Fire burned under my skin.

I'm mad I may be losing my mother, and this was the way we finally connected. I'm mad Stacey is gone. I'm mad my heart is so confused about three men. I'm mad I must marry in order to lead. I'm just so damn mad.

Now I understand why Mother refused to have special connections to anyone. It's too dam hard caring about people. I had to calm down before I burned down everything in my room.

I gazed to the floor at the stuff I flung to the floor. Coming across the envelope T-B-N gave me days ago. Something told me to leave it where it was, but my curiosity got the best of me.

I had forgotten all about it. I picked it up and broke the seal. Two truths and a lie, and a letter to our younger self.

Side One:

1. I once met death, but miraculously survived when I was in crossover.
2. My first kiss was with a girl name Beatrice. We were four.
3. The first time I killed a person. I was twelve.

Side Two:

Dear Young James,

Never be afraid to love. Never cower. Never run. Never hide. Stand up straight and look your fears in its face. Always remember the man you become is only built from the character of the boy you molded yourself to be. Cherish *every second with your mother. She will fade early, and all you will have left are her memories.*

P.S. When you meet a girl named Katianna. She will be leader of Blue. You will fall for her before you even know her, and when you take her on a first day, you will fall even more. Don't run. Stay. Fight for her heart.

I grabbed the quill and circled the ones I thought were truths. Leaving the one I thought was lie, alone.

I believed two and three are truths, and ones a lie. It's not uncommon for a boy at the age of twelve to have witnessed death or even have killed himself.

I know boys younger than that who already shed blood on their daddies' swords. It's just the way they were. We live in a dog-eat-dog world.

I sat there wondering what he circled on my paper, and what he thought of my letter to my younger self. He certainly raises my eyebrow.

I wanted to dislike him more after our date, but I grew a tiny inkling of admiration.

Hearing his story and seeing the sweet side of him that no one else gets to see because he always portrays himself to be a strong man with no feelings.

Now, I realized, he hurts just like the rest of us. His heart has feelings. I still didn't fully trust him. From what I gather, he was raised by his father. A very powerful man in Black.

His father is Blacks leader-right hand man. They are a wealthy family with great stature. They're responsible for the bulk of trades. Marrying him will be the strongest alliance for Blue.

Not just for trades, but for their armies. They house Vikings and pirates. Both very dominant.

To gain Black, will make us the most powerful Village. Mother already has ties with Black.

There's no telling if it meant they will have ties to me. Once a leader steps down, many Villages switch off.

TWENTY-THREE

KATIANNA

Dinner was set. I sent guards to find Thomas. He was found throwing axes out back. The guards stated that he'd be joining soon. That he wanted to freshen up. I had Victoria make a room for him. Hoping he'd decided to stay.

Running into Lee was the last thing I expected when roaming through the pillars. He was leaned up against one. I stopped in my tracks when I stumbled upon him. It was weird though. It was as if I hadn't stopped, he would have let me keep going. "Lee, hello. Joining for dinner?" I asked.

"No thank you. I don't have much of an appetite these days."

"Don't be like that."

"Be like what? You expect me to sit happily at the dinner table watching you blush for not one, but now two other men." I attempted to storm off before he grabbed at my arm. I knew exactly what he was getting at. "I'm sorry. I didn't mean it like that. But can you imagine how I feel." He forced me to look him in the eyes. "Just days ago, we had a moment in the kitchen. You went off on a date, and days later invited another man back to Village. I'm competing with two others. It was bad enough when it was just one. You suppose I fourth wheel."

"I supposed nothing. If you won't eat, that's on you. And there is no competition. I belong to no one. I told you before I could never be yours." He pulled me hard into his arm. "Then why'd you kiss me, why'd you come all over my fingers and watch me lick it off?"

I gulped hard in my throat. Electricity stirred in my veins. Although I'm learning to control it. I can tell by the way I made it settle.

"It was a moment of weakness. It won't happen again. I assure you." I pushed my arms off his grip and walked away.

I knew he was watching me. I knew he was hurting. I'm hurting to. I never meant for things to become this way between us. Especially us.

Why'd I have to go running behind him that day. Now it seems we can't be friends.

I wish things could go back to the way they were. I have hope that maybe one day it will. Me pretending that I don't feel what he feels, bothers me more than he knows. I'm trying to protect everyone's heart, including my own.

To choose, meant to break someone's heart. And that'll break my heart as well.

Moments later, Thomas entered the dining hall. The scent of his masculinity wisped in the air.

The scent was woodsy, leathery, with a touch of bergamot. I'd never smelled cologne on him before. He never wore it when we spent time in the woods. It heightened the senses in my nostrils.

Since I've been gifted. My powers cause delicacy to my body. I see things differently. Clearer. Everything I touch, I feel it in my bones.

As he walked pass, ladies fawned over him. Chuckling and whispering in each other's ears. It made me smile knowing they fawned over him, but he fawned over me.

Not that I wanted it to happen, but maybe, just maybe, he'd take interest in one of the ladies here in court.

Of course, it meant I won't have him, but at least he'd be here. That thought faltered the moment he placed a kiss on my cheek in greeting me.

Taking a seat to the left side of me. His damn eyes are so beautiful. Dessert storm against my green lands.

We spent the entire dinner talking with each other. It was a completely rude thing to do. Ignoring everyone around us. But that's how I felt when I was near him. Like no one else was around.

I guess it was something we've mastered the art of in the woods. He's the one who taught it to me. He's the one who helped me pass challenge.

The new information I now know about him, changed the dynamic of everything. I felt even closer to him. Knowing, he too, is a leader. Maybe not of an actual Village, but a leader none the less.

Lee never showed up to dinner. I'm not sure why I had hope that he would. Afterall, he was right.

Who would want to sit at a table and eat while watching the one they love interact with another.

It was upsetting. I know I lead him on. I lead everyone on. I give each one of them hope in a way that makes them believe they could be with me.

Even if I didn't say it directly. It was still that. Every kiss, every touch, every blush that spreads on my face. It was hope. I must stop giving hope. I fear one day it will lead to death.

"Stay." I pleaded with Thomas.

He smiled at me. "I can't do that."

"Just until tomorrow. I need you as witness when Willow goes to hearing. You were there. Your knowledge can help render judgment."

"I could always come back tomorrow for that. I'm only a few miles away."

"Yes, of course." I smiled in defeat. Thomas was harder than the others. He didn't fall at my feet like T-B-N, or Lee. With Thomas, I had to work for his attention, and that only did one thing. It made me want him more.

Stop it. Stop it. Stop it. No hope.

****

When I retired to my chambers. Victoria was already waiting inside. I'd been wanting to speak with her. Since she's been acting weird lately.

"Are you feeling well today?" I asked as I started undressing. She skipped to me to help me out. Untying laces from the back of my dress.

"I'm just fine my lady."

"Hmm. Good." My gown hit the floor, and her gaze landed to my breasts. Immediate embarrassment took over her face when she'd seen I saw her looking. She jumped back. "Sorry. I wasn't…..I." I grabbed her hands. "Victoria. Breathe. No harm, no foul." She smiled. "You're such a kind leader."

Those words pierced through me like a dagger. I knew she meant it as in to say my mother wasn't.

People feared The Mother. That's not something I wish to have.

If people fear you, it means they'd be afraid to come to you. They'd make stupid decisions just off the fact of being so afraid.

I wanted people to trust me. To come to me even if they felt they'd be punished. It showed more character. It'll make me rule with more compassion and take into consideration their courage.

"Have you an answer for me?"

"An answer about what my lady?"

"About what I asked you before." She looked confused. "About you moving into Court with your little sisters." Her eyebrows furrowed discerningly.

"My lady. I have no siblings. I am an only child."

My mind raced at her words. Maybe I heard wrong. Maybe at that time my powers were deceiving me. Causing me to imagine things.

Whatever the case, there was something more to be told. Either she's hiding something, or I'm out of my mind. Always bet on the house.

Moments after Victoria left my chambers. I heard noises at the window. Someone was throwing pebbles. There was only one person who'd had ever done that.

"What is it." I shouted as I tilted my head down after I opened the window.

"Can we talk. You promised me."

"Can it wait until tomorrow. I am ready for bed."

"It won't take long."

Why does this man annoy me the most. "And how do you suppose I sneak out. There are guards outside my door." He nodded his head to the window then to the wall. "You're kidding me right…. you expect me to sneak out the window. I am a leader. I don't climb out windows."

"You are a skillful climber. I know you can do it with your eyes closed." He folded his arms. "You aren't scared, are you? don't worry I'll catch you if you fall." He smirked. It annoyed the shit out of me.

He knew what he was doing. He knew I hated being called out. I bit my bottom lip and rolled my eyes. For some reason, I just know I'm going to regret doing this.

I stepped out onto the ledge facing backwards. So that the front of my body aligned to the wall. I planted my feet on the first solid rock.

Concertation consumed me. I scaled these same exactly walls before. Plenty of times when I was young. Sneaking out at night with Stacey.

It's been a while since I've had to do so. I paced myself taking and letting out short breaths. "That's it, you got it." He shouted from below. "Shut up." I countered.

I slipped a bit, misplacing my right footing. I quickly caught my balance as I shifted my body to the left.

My fingernails dug into the rocks as if I were holding on for dear life. I remembered it being much easier back then. I'd scale with zero problems.

I guess those days are long gone. My nineteen-year-old, soon to be twenty-year-old body, begged to differ. "Almost there." He alarmed me.

Which came in handy because I felt like I was taking too long.

I could have channeled my earth manipulation to get me down, but I wanted to challenge myself without powers.

Mother told me not to channel unless I had to. Besides, I'm sure I'll have to use it to climb back up when I come back.

If it's this hard going down, I'm sure as hell, won't make it back up without help.

He placed his hand on me when I came closer to the ground. "Hands off ass.....off ass now." I stilled until he stepped back.

I jumped down the rest of the way. Nearly breaking my fall. He stepped back with his hands high in the air.

"Now." I brush dirt off my clothes. "What was so important and couldn't wait until tomorrow, that I had to climb out a window this late at night."

He smiled at me. As if my anger enlightened him. He took out the envelope we made on our date. "And that is what couldn't wait until tomorrow?"

I raised my eyebrows in disappointment. He's worse than a begging child.

"No, it couldn't. It's important to me. I'd lose sleep if I had to go another night without knowing."

"Fine." We began walking. Ducking and dodging every corner that stood guards. I must admit. This is kind of fun. Sneaking out. On the verge of trouble.

The thrill of being caught. It made my adrenaline rush. I'd never admit it to him though. We walked until we found the only spot nobody inhabited.

The Willow tree. He took of his rucksack unzipping it, pulling out a blanket for us to sit on. "I can't stay long. You said it would be quick." I gazed around at all the content he displayed. Berries and cheeses.

A lot of similar things from our picnic, without the wine. "It won't be long. But for however long I am able to have your company. I'd rather you be full."

I rolled my eyes and folded my arms.

"Ladies first." I made him look the other direction as I lifted my shirt pulling the folded paper from my bra.

We exchanged papers. Laughing at the same time of the answers we each gave. "Why are you laughing?" I asked. "I'm laughing at your answers.

My two truths are one and three. Two was a lie." I was shocked. Not at the answer with him killing someone at age twelve, but at the answer about him seeing death. I had to know more. I asked him to elaborate.

"When I was seven, my mother took me for a swim by the ocean. When she turned her back, I went in to deep after she'd told me to stay put. Only the waves were too strong for my little body. I screamed for help. Until I couldn't. Water had filled my lungs. I was sure I was a goner. I saw darkness at first. I crossed over. I saw things that told me so. My spirit entered another realm. I spent time in heaven. I saw my grandparents and others who we lost. Then I woke up, gagging water out my mouth. My father had saved me. Apparently, he followed us to the ocean. Days later when I told my mother what I saw and who I saw describing them from what I remembered. She told me I saw my grandparents. I'd never seen them, or even seen a picture of them before."

"Wow." Was all I could say. We sat in silence for a few minutes.

"Well if it's any consolation, you picked my truths and lie correctly. Two and three are the ones." He laughed saying "I knew it." Patting himself on the back. I began to think I was easily predictable.

"The letter to your younger self was powerful. I admire you so much for it." He admitted.

"Yours was interesting and meaningful as well." I complimented.

"I'd like us to keep each other's paper, if you don't mind."

"I don't mind at all." I folded the paper perfectly back into its previous folds and set it back where I pulled it from.

Time slipped away as we talked more and more. Next thing I know, the sun was rising, and I was wiping my eyes.

"James, get up." I shoved at him. "We fell asleep. I have to get back before I'm found out." He began sitting up, wiping at his eyes as well.

"You've done nothing wrong."

"Done nothing wrong……I've done everything wrong." With nothing to gather I began to run. He didn't run after me.

Knowing it was pointless to do so. I channeled earth using the vines to give me leverage to crawl upwards.

Panting stole my breathes as I panicked to desperately go faster, unnoticed. I made it up and into the windows. Crawling in from the ledge backwards. Nearly sending my soul outside my body when I saw a shadowy figure from the walls of my room.

Father was at my bed. His face was unreadable. I couldn't tell if he was mad, concerned, sad, or what. I wonder how long he'd been here.

"Father…I…is everything ok?" Tears rolled down his eyes and I knew everything was not ok. I knew what was wrong. My channeled spirit told me so. It was death. Mother was gone.

I felt the same feeling I had when I first learned of Stacey's death.

Father had the same empty look in his eyes Lee did. I dropped top my knees before him and screamed. I cried so hard; water channeled.

The ground rumbled as I whaled. I could feel the force of nature as the waves stood high in the ocean. I couldn't control it. I didn't want to hurt anyone. If there was anyone near the waters, they'd be in big trouble right now.

Father placed his hands on the back of my head as I cried into his lap. I rocked back and forth.

He stood up and dropped to the floor with me. We cried together.

No matter how much anger I felt towards her for not loving me the way I wanted to be love. It still hurt, nonetheless. She was my mother. She raised me, she trained me, she taught me almost everything I knew.

My heart sunk to the bottom of the ocean. I have no idea how long I'd been screaming, all I knew was that I cried so hard, I had no more tears left. They faded.

I screamed so hard, I had no voice, it faded. I should have been the one comforting my father. It is his wife he lost. Instead, he comforted me.

"It's ok, it's ok, it's ok, it's ok bunny. It's ok." He tried his best to calm me. He hasn't called me bunny since I was fifteen and begged him to stop because it embarrassed me.

Hearing him call me that now after all these years, made my heart hurt more.

"I'm sorry. I…" I couldn't breathe. He held me in his arms. I didn't have to speak. He didn't have to speak. We shared the pain equally.

The bell rang loud outside. Alarming Villagers that we lost a leader. Whenever the bell rings, that particular bell. It meant we had a fallen leader.

I could already hear people frantic. They were confused if it was the signal of the old leader or the new one. Being that it was the same bell for both. I couldn't leave my father's side as he grieved. I sent for Victoria.

"My mother has fallen. Let the people know. No one is to come in or out mine or my fathers' chambers. No one. We ask for privacy as we grieve. Until I say so."

Victoria stood there with tears in her eyes. Sympathy dripped from her body as her head tilted and her eyebrows furrowed.

She didn't speak one word, but I knew she was sorry. She stood still a moment too long. Like she was stuck in a trance.

The inside of being wanted to shoo her away, but somehow her eyes got the best of me.

Apart of my abilities, shall I channel deep enough, is the reading of people's minds through their eyes. It made perfect sense to me being that I was always a person who sought out feelings through the eyes.

They tell the deepest stories and darkest secrets. Victoria finally left and I knew dark days were ahead of me. Ahead of us all.

My mother was by far the toughest women I had ever met, and still, my heart bleeds for her. She didn't deserve this. No one does. I wish.

My only wish is that people only died of old age. Not from being tortured, murdered, sickly, or any other brutal mortalities.

People respected The Mother. Maybe fear had a lot to do with it. She was always so impatient and short tempered. The kind of person who didn't think twice about the deliveries of one's consequences. She didn't need time to think about it.

TWENTY-FOUR

KATIANNA

I layed on my back, on the floor. Staring up at the ceiling. It's been hours since I left father.

When I left him. I ordered the return of my little brothers. Whom she sent them away safely when Blue was attacked.

I wondered why she never sent for them once everything was cleared. It made me think she kept them away for a reason.

Maybe she knew she was dying and didn't want them to be sad for her. To stick around and witness. I have nothing but thoughts swarming around in my head as I lay here.

My back started to hurt causing me to shift position. The more I shifted, the more it hurt.

Maybe I wanted to feel the pain. Maybe if I suffered it made me feel better. To be happy, comfortable, or to enjoy any form of life would make me feel guilty.

Silent burning tears fell down my face. Melting tiny holes into the ground as they fell off my face onto the floor. I could care less about anything right now.

Of course, death is a part of life, and one day I knew my parents will someday be gone. But I still never expected it. I hadn't expected it to be this sad, this weird.

Life is funny that way, I guess. I could have been prepared to the max for this day to come, and it still would hurt no less.

My poor little brothers. Growing up with a stern mother was better than growing up with no mother at all.

She will never see me married. Never see me have children. She will never get to see how great I'm going to rule in honor of her name.

I tried to channel my spirit realm. Hoping I'd receive some sort of message from the other world. Hoping she'd appear to me.

To tell me none of its real. To tell me everything's going to be alright. The harder I concentrated, the further away from success I was.

I hate that I have yet mastered the art of my powers.

A knock on the door broke my daze. I immediately stiffened on the floor. Who would be so stupid to interrupt me. Everyone knew better.

But apparently not, because some fool who doesn't care about his or her own death is asking for what's about to come.

The knock was soft. Barely there. Whoever it was, treaded lightly. I gathered myself up, sighing at the pain that caught up to my body when I got up too fast.

My knees cracked and my back barely allowed me to stand fully straight. I announced through the door. "Go away."

"Never will I ever go away. Open the door, Princess."

My pulse began to race as the immediate sound of his voice had effects, I never realized they had. I slowly unlocked the door.

Never opening it for him, but the sound of the lock unlocking was enough to let him know he was welcomed.

I didn't know how to feel about him being here. If it would be anyone to be so brave to disturb me, it would be him.

That means he knows my heart bleeds for him. And it does. He's the bestest friend I ever had next to Stacey.

It's always been the three of us. He opened the door. Swinging it slowly. Once inside, he locked it back.

"Remind me to fire the guards." I said in a way that I'm sure he wondered if it were a joke. Only it wasn't.

I took my place back on the floor. Pain and all. Pain is all I want to feel. He took up a space right next to me. Laying down on his back, on the floor.

We said nothing to each other. He never even looked at me. He was just there. We stayed like that for I assume to be several hours. I turned my body.

It was my desperate attempt to change position. He followed the notion. Maybe he thought I did it as a gesture.

Whatever the case, we were facing each other now. He cupped my face in his hands. "You can be weak in front of me. I promise I'll act as if it never happened." The tears immediately ran down my face.

I controlled it enough so that it came out as regular tears. Not the burning rain drops.

A funny feeling took over my body as I made a mental note of how I was able to do so. It felt good though. Being me.

Being a regular human with no powers, crying regular tears. He pulled my body closer to his. Forcing me to lay my head on his chest. His chest was firm but just right. His heartbeat was fast.

The scent of his clean hair immediately settled its home in my lungs.

His arms were enveloped around me. It felt good. In this moment ironically, I couldn't imagine being in anyone else's arms besides him.

I wanted it to be him. Maybe he's, my person. Or maybe it was the deeper connection I had to him than the others.

He grew up in my mother's care. He knew her just as much as I. The others only maybe knew her for a short time. Especially Thomas. He didn't know her at all.

Whatever the case, I just know I love Lee. "Life is not promised tomorrow." I could feel his chin burrow down at my words. He was looking at me under his eyes.

"That's something she would always say to me. And I know it only means to cherish moments. To live now." I shifted in his arms, pulling myself up a little to face him. "Lee. I.."

He stopped me. "Don't." He paused. "All I want is to be here for you. No pressure, no decisions, no judgements." He kissed my forehead. "Lay back down." He practically forced my head down to his chest. I tried desperately to keep my eyes open. I'm sure it's the middle of the night when I shifted under Lees arms.

Peeling my heavy eyelids open so that I could get up to use the garderobe. Lee groaned at my movements, but he never woke.

He rolled on the floor as if he was relieved of the pressure my head once weighed against his chest. He looked peaceful.

When I opened the door, Thomas was sitting with his back leaned against the frame. Nearly falling all the way back. I jumped in surprised when his body leaned against my feet. Clearly, he had been sleeping.

I helped gather him up closing the door behind us. When he landed his eyes on mines, he smiled a half smile.

The guards gave explanation as soon as I looked to them. "Sorry my Lady, he refused to leave. He threatened to kill us." Terror seeped in his eyes, and it made me wonder if Thomas channeled and it was enough to scare them. "He was at your door all night until he sat down an hour ago." I gave a nod to Sir William letting him know it was ok.

I'm guessing, they knew what he meant to me as well. I was starting to question if my hidden feelings for all my men were a secret at all.

It appears everyone knows exactly what my heart feels. As if it were plastered across my sleeve where I wear it.

We walked in the direction of the hall leading to where I so desperately needed to be. I felt the arousal of it way before Lee came to my chambers, but I was numb. I'm certainly paying the price for it now.

We spoke no words on the way there. I love that about him. It's as if he knows when to speak and when not to. He was leaned against the wall when I finished. His eyes were now fully awoken. He was him.

"Hi." I spoke.

"Hi." He countered. "Come here." He held his arms out beckoning my body.

Tears formed all over again before I even buried my face in his chest. I hate crying. I hate being an emotional wreck.

I spent my whole life avoiding tears. Somehow these past few weeks, it's all I ever do.

Mother always taught me that tears were a sign of weakness. She told me to never let them see you cry. I'd always asked her "Who?" She'd always say "Whoever." She was tougher than I am, I give her that.

I don't have the same outlook on crying as she did. I would secretly cry in my room at night under my blanket so she wouldn't know. It wouldn't be for a specific reason.

I used to force myself to cry, just so I know what it felt like. Until one day I got hurt running outside with Stacey.

I tripped and gashed my knee open on a sharp-edged rock that seemed to have come out of nowhere. When I was sent to the infirmary to be stitched. I cried.

When she entered the infirmary, she immediately forbad my tears.

Even the nurses who attended to my wounds tried to tell her that I was just a little girl in pain, and it was ok for me to cry because it hurted. Mother caused an uproar.

The poor lady, whose name I can't remember, was sent the hole for punishment. I never understood why Mother did that.

I was even more confused when she had my brothers, how she allowed them to be human. In the way she never allowed me.

They cried plenty of times. She even babied them when they did so. That's why when she told me I was her favorite when she was dying, I didn't believe it. How could I be.

Thomas held me. We stayed in the halls, holding onto each other.

"When I arrived at your Chambers, I was told I could not enter. I threatened your guards and in return the allowed me passage. One of them warned me that you were not alone. I nearly beat it out of him to tell me who you were with. When I was informed, I backed off. I didn't want to intrude. However, there's not a chance in this world that I would have left without seeing if you were ok for myself. So here I am."

My words were stuck in my throat. Maybe they were stuck in my brain. I hadn't a clue what I should be saying back to him. I was dealing with enough emotions as is. But I had to say something. Anything. Say something.

"Thomas. I know this is weird. I know what it looks like. Lee came just to grieve with me. He and I are childhood friends. Nothing happened between us." He released his hold on me.

"You're hurting, we don't have to go there if you're not ready."

I figured I ripped the band aid off now. Rather than endure more pain and open wounds later. *Give me all the hurt now.* "No. It's ok. I would like to talk about it now." He stepped aside extending his arm so that I would lead us to wherever I wanted to go talk.

The Kitchen was the only thing on my mind. I so desperately needed to wet my throat. Once we arrived and I gave us both glasses of water.

We sat at the oldest wooden table. I have no clue why I picked it. I have a weird thing about loving old things. Things people forget about because they're not shiny and new anymore.

I sucked in a deep breath, closing my eyes while I talked. "I know this is a weird situation to have walked in on. I know we only met months ago. We shared a moment." I held his gaze as I felt the burn of his stare on my cheek. "And it was a special moment. It's not fair to ask you to stay and drag you into my shit, but I selfishly ask you anyway. Because now that I do know you. My heart won't give you up."

He nodded his head up and down. "But your heart won't give him up either." My elbow knocked itself off the table at his statement. "I know we both had lives before we met each other, and I know there are others who may have already been fond of you before me. I ask nothing of you. Only that we remain close, because my heart won't give you up either, and I rather have you as a friend than nothing at all. I. Will. Always. Love. You. I'm not mad." He placed his hand on my face, and I sank into his touch.

"Thank You." I kissed his cheek.

"Get up." He stood and reached his hand out to grab mine. I had no clue why, but I reached. He walked us to where the kitchen maid keeps their music. He turned on music.

"We're going to battle."

"Battle." I said in confusion. Looking at him like he had two heads.

"Yes, were going to dance battle. Winner gets to choose one thing they want the other to do, and they can't say no. Even if it's the most ridiculous request."

I'm confused but so very much intrigued. It's the middle of the night and he wants to dance battle in the kitchen.

He broke away from me clearly starting by dancing first. The music was upbeat. So different than the normal sad dance body to body music that usually plays.

He brung his hand up to his chest as if he were about to make a pledge. Then he began footwork. Stepping in sync to the beat of the music.

He shifted his body all around. My eyes were dizzy from all the directions I had to look. He looked completely silly. He can't dance at all. Not like T-B-N, for sure.

He was running in and out of tables. Crossing across the floor.

It made me laugh. I got lost in it. Not thinking of anyone, not even my mother's death.

He made me forget, if even just for a little while. It's why I love him back. Because of shit like this. Although I could never tell him. When he called himself being done, he was panting slightly.

His chest and shoulders rose up and down in synchronization. He pointed his finger at me. It was a challenge. It was my go.

I didn't prance like a sweet girl. I was anything but. I threw my arms up and jumped on the table. I then jumped table to table, doing dances at each one I jumped to.

He stared at me smiling. Shaking his head. I'm sure I look ridiculous. When I jumped down to finish, I almost fell, and he was right there to catch me.

While he held me halfway leaning back from catching me. I stood in his arms panting heavier than he did when he finished, meanwhile I did less.

For some reason, I didn't fix myself. I didn't move. "I think it's safe to say I won." He said winking down at me. "I beg to differ." He smiled at my disapproval. "Shall we go again." He offered. I thought about it.

I don't think my body can physically go again, and deep down I knew he won. "Ok fine, you win. What is it that you want." I asked still leaned back laying his arms. The arms that didn't fix itself to let me up just as much as I didn't fix myself to sit up. "Kiss me." My heart constricted at his demand.

I was nervous. As if we never kissed before, as if I didn't want to, knowing I did. "But not right now." My nervous eyes turned to dark confusion. "Kiss me when you fall in love with me. Because you will one day feel for me what I feel for you." *Oh, Thomas I already do.* I just can't tell you.

An abrupt noise from the other side of the kitchen broke our trance.

Thomas quickly ran to the table to retrieve the sword he placed there before we danced. My senses immediately channeled.

The slightest hint of danger brings the pyrokinesis out of me. It must be my favorite one. Thomas extended his arm to tell me to stay back as he faintly walked to where the noise was coming from.

How daring of Thomas. His first instinct is to protect, meanwhile I can wield any power I want. Even though I have more powers than him.

His need to protect me is one of the most attractive things I like about him. The way he doesn't give up. The way he not too long ago stayed outside my bedroom even though he knew I was inside with another, and still wanted nothing but to make sure I was ok.

I don't think no one will truly understand the bond I've built with him. Or the bond I built with T-B-N, ironically.

More noise protruded the same area. It was too loud a noise to be a rat. His sword was ready for blood. I wondered if he would channel his wolf.

I wonder if he now knew how to control it. I made a mental note to ask him about it later. Maybe he could teach me what he knew. Victoria crept out the dark corner, the closer we neared. "Victoria." I uttered as she stepped forward.

"I'm so sorry my lady. Please forgive me. I was so thirsty for a drink of water. Then I realized I was quite hungry as well. I know no one is allowed in the kitchen off hours. When I heard people coming. I hid. When I realized it was you, I got too nervous and embarrassed to show my face." She was shaking. Her eyes looked as if they'd seen a ghost.

She looked confused at her own answers. Maybe she knew it didn't make much sense, and that she could have come up with a better lie.

However, I felt terrible. I know there's something up with her.

My first thoughts were that she was either spying on me, or that she was secretly in love with me. I remembered how I caught her staring at my body.

I've caught her other times as well. Stealing glances, and lingering touches. The way she brushed my hair. The way she traced her hands on my shoulders when she washed my back.

Either way I'm going to launch my own investigation. Thomas and I held each other's gaze as we volleyed. "Just go." I told her. "We'll deal with this later." She ran off without hesitation.

"That was strange." Thomas stated.

"Very." I shook my head in agreeance.

I had a lot on my plate to be focusing on Victoria's weirdness. I will however, in the coming days, hosting auditions and background checks for new ladies.

Maybe it's time to rip off the band-aid. Thomas escorted me back to my chambers. I asked him if he would come to Mothers arrangements. Which is also something I have to deal with. He assured me he would.

Upon walking in my chambers. Lee was awake. Sitting up on the floor with his back leaned the footboard frame.

I don't know why I was hoping to be lucky enough that he'd be still asleep when I returned. Luck hasn't been on my side in a while. Still, I hoped. Foolish hope maybe. Who the hell sleeps for that long. I was missing for quite some time.

"That was a lot of liquid you poured." He couldn't even look up at me. His sarcastic tone of voice told me exactly what he was referring to. He must have asked the guards where I went, or maybe he followed me himself. Maybe he saw me dancing in the kitchen.

"Yes, well when nature calls. I also got tied up in other things."

"Hmmm." He sighed in sarcasm. "Tied up in other things in the middle of the night."

"Yes. It happens. I am a leader of an entire Village. Shit happens in the middle of the night sometimes." I don't know why I just said that. The guilty conscious in me took over.

He grabbed his hand on the footboard to help bring himself to his feet. He walked towards me. "Well. I'm glad you're feeling better. It's enough to make me wanna dance." He broke the closeness between us.

Stepping aside from me and gearing towards the door. I didn't stop him. Nor did I say anything in counter to his sarcasm.

I felt bad, but I told him just as I told the others. I belong to no one. And if him being there for me made him think he had some sort of claim on me. Well then, I bets keep my distance.

Next time I'll console myself. I'll reject his sympathy. I'm trying my hardest not to hurt anyone of them. I know their positions in this isn't easy. But my leadership comes first.

TWENTY-FIVE

LEE

She thinks she knows the pain I feel. She doesn't. Nobody does. Not even her other interests. I spent the night on a hard cold floor to be there for her. I am always there for her. Just to have hear continuously rip my heart out of chest.

She spent hours dancing and having special moments with a man nobody even knows. She ran off to the woods and came back with this stranger.

They call him Thomas. She won't even talk to me about their exact relationship or where he even came from. She's too trusting of people, and it bothers me.

The more she trusts people, the less sleep I get. Because it's the more time I have to spend digging for secrets and protecting her.

And trust me, I will dig up every single one of his secrets. The same way I dug of David's. Just wait until her father hears about that. I'm good at what I do.

Did I ever imagine this is what'd I'd be spending my days doing? Of course not. But when you find something your good at, it becomes your craft. You become a master of its art.

All I needed was one last piece of information to confirm what I know about David. As soon as that's all over. I'll be working on this fake Thomas guy. The nerve of her.

It was quiet near the stone walls. It's never quiet here. There are always children playing nearby. Always commotion going on, being that it's one of the recreation areas.

The silence is unnerving. I crept slowly around the pillar to take a peek before I stepped openly to the center.

Once the coast was clear I shuffled quickly through to the ending passage. There was no sign of danger, no sign of life either.

Suddenly Katiannas lady's maid Victoria appeared out of the shadows. Causing me to stump backwards out of startle. She tilted her head at me as if I was just the person she was looking for. "Out here alone. How unlikely." She tilted her head in the opposite direction.

The strangeness split the air thick between us. It was an odd comment to make. I'm always alone.

Why she'd care anyway. I ignored her and continued walking. "She'll never choose you. She doesn't look at you the way she looks at him." My attention immediately stopped me in my tracks.

"What'd you just say?" I turned around to face her.

"You heard me quite well. You just don't care for the truth. Trapped bunny in a rabbit's cage." Her head tilted back and forth. She looked like a derange person.

I wasn't sure if she knew something I didn't know, if she was trying to hurt me, or if she was trying to hurt Katianna. Either way I don't take lightly to threats. Whether direct or indirect.

I got closer, grabbed her by her wrist. Gripping it the tightest my cold dead hands would allow. "Be careful of the foolish things you spit from your tongue. You don't want to go through life not being able to ever speak again because your mouth misses it main source." I held her gaze. Anger looking at anger. "How will you eat." I added. She looked to me unbothered by my dominance. Instead, she giggled like a maniac.

Her pupils dilated. Whatever drugs she's on surely is getting the best of her.

She continued laughing even when I turned my back to walk away. Maybe she was the reason no one occupied the area of the stone walls. Perhaps the children were afraid of her. Perhaps she's been out here scaring people. Another person I'll have to investigate.

I requested a meeting with Joe to update him on the powerful information I now have concerning his behavior and whereabouts. It will be perfect timing.

The last piece of information I was waiting on finally arrived in my hands just moments ago.

Awhile after my run in with weird-toria. Until then I'll keep my head down.

If Katianna doesn't fall in love with me after this, then I don't know what will make her do so.

I don't expect her to jump into my arms, falling hopelessly in love, but I expect she will show me gratitude.

That she will finally see I'll go to the end of the world for her. Hell, I'll end the world for her.

****

"What news do you bring?" Joe asked as we sat opposite side in the meeting room.

We sat so far apart even though there was no one else in the room. I slid the envelope across the table to him.

He caught it just in time before it slipped off the table. His eyes widened with shock and then sadness as they filled with tears.

He covered his mouth with his hand. "Is this certain?" He asked glaring at me as if he had to ask. Deep down he knew me and what I'm capable of. It's why he chose me to captain a ship when we searched for his daughter.

He knew the information before was nothing but truth. "For how long?"

"Ever since I started following him, I suppose. But I suppose it was even before that."

"How did you come to find this?"

"I had my people test it. The results were positive. I got the reports from the autopsy puled this afternoon. Sir, the results coincided with my speculations as well as the berries he picked and buried. He poisoned Lady Mary-Ann. He killed your wife." He cringed and crumbled the papers in his hands at the truth I spoke.

"I'm so sorry," My heart felt for Joe. For Katianna too. Even though we're not quite friendly at the moment. My only wish is that he pays for the consequences of his actions.

I'm sure the daughter of the women he murdered will render him a fair judgement. I'm sure the people will understand why he took the life of their leader, and deceived everyone into thinking she was sick.

This trauma will wreak havoc for us all when. Katianna finds out, and may God be with us all when it does.

I selfishly couldn't help but wonder if she will cry on my chest. If she will let me hold her into the night.

There was still piece of me that held onto a sliver of hope for us. She's just confused. Joe was long gone as I sat here in my thoughts.

I imagine he's out for blood. That he summoned the guards, sounded the traitor alarm, and he was probably on his way to David's chambers.

The report was clear about her death being the result of being poisoned. Her fingernails were black, and they found multiple clots in her brain.

What has the world come to when even the closet person to you, can kill you so easily. It's sick. People are sick in the head. Maybe I am too.

My obsession with Katianna is consuming my every thought. Even when I temporarily think of other things, there isn't a moment that goes by where I don't find a way to add her into whatever it is I'm thinking about.

Maybe the only way to have her, is to get rid of those who stand in my way. If what Joe promised me doesn't work, then it's something I just may have to consider.

I'll spill all the blood for her. She's mine.

TWENTY-SIX

KATIANNA

Father burst through my chambers. Prior to, I heard commotion outside my doors. I was already alert.

My daggers in hand. I set them down when I realized who it was. His eyes were red. He seemed distorted. It took only moments before he told me what's happened.

He said that David, my mother's right hand was behind her death. Said that he's to be implemented for poisoning. Confusion took over.

How could this be. They were childhood friends. That's like Lee one day being responsible for my death.

We may be at odds at the moment, but I know he would never do anything to hurt me.

David was at mothers' side daily. There must be some reasonable explanation. Or it was a lie all together. Either way, I ordered him to the black hole until a full investigation concluded. Father wanted me to have his head.

I'm sure that's what I would want as well, but this is the thing about being a leader. You have to make decisions based on truths, facts, and evidence, and right now, this was just hearsay. If this turns out to be true, I will certainly have more than his head. That wouldn't be punishment enough. He'll suffer, and so will his wife.

For now, we wait. Wait until there's a trial hearing. Which is tomorrow. I still must get through today's hearing with that nutty bitch Willow who tried to kill me with her shapeshifting.

I received word that she's allowed a panel of ten people from her Village at her side. Playing by the rules irked me in more ways than one. However, it is a rule I must follow.

Sitting on the throne awaiting parliament and the attendees of the people to file in, I couldn't help but think about the news father brought to me only moments ago.

I kept replaying in my head any scenarios where I questioned David's intentions with my mother. I kept coming up empty handed.

Except the one time when I was at her side, and he came into interrupt telling me it was time for her to take her medication.

It was a simple thing, but I felt something that day. Something unnerving settled in my stomach. It was the way he said it, the way he looked.

It was almost as if he was in a hurry to feed her the medicine. As if he was afraid, she'd come to.

The room filled with everyone needed to begin. A smirky look on Willows face annoyed my entire being. So much that the fire boiled in my blood.

Rising in tension. I wanted nothing more than to smack the smirk off her face. I gazed to the audience where I saw Lee, T-B-N, and Thomas all in attendance. Sitting separately of course, but still. I'm smiling on the inside, but I can show no favor to one in particular.

Even though my heart skipped a beat at the sight of one in particular. I wondered if it meant I've chosen.

"Willow of white. You've come to my Village and try to take my life. Speak your truth before I render judgment. You should know that the attempt on another leader's life is grounds for treason." I clean picked in my nails out of boredom and my lack of compassion for whatever lies that are about to spill from her mouth.

Her ten chosen panel fidgeted and whispered in their seats. Her father, former leader, the twins Mia and Maya included.

"I know your secrets. Let me go now and maybe I'll spare you."

My head tilted in complete and utter shock at how easy she thinks this must be. She's making a mockery of me in my own Court.

"I have a million actual important things to do. I have no secrets. Stop embarrassing yourself and get on with it before I condemn you to your death. My patience is wearing thin."

"Katianna of Blue." She shouted into the crowd. "She was wrongfully gifted her powers. Her dead mother made a deal with the devil. That is why she's dead. She sold her soul so that her daughter would take over with multiple powers and become the strongest of all. No one is that lucky to have been blessed with the powers of an all-in-one spiriter. She's a witch."

The room grew stentorian. People were gasping, whispering, shouting, pointing, and confused. As they looked every which way.

"Order." Mr. Punic shouted.

"She tells nothing but lies. She's a freak. It's her ploy to get out of the trouble she caused. It has nothing to do with why she's here. She attempted my life. For that reason, I order her death."

Ten members shouted, stood up, cursed, and spit on my sacred floors. I knew White Villagers were crazy, but these people have gone mad.

"I tell no lies. I have a witness. Only he is not here."

"How convenient." I stated.

"He's not here because she ordered him to the black hole. His name is David. He was her mother's henchman." She looked up at me. My eyes burned fire. I know their red. I'm trying to control what my reactions are. Father looked at me in delusion.

"Bring forth the witness." Mr. Punic said. My eyes gazed to him as I realized him ordering David's appearance only meant one thing. It meant that he didn't trust me.

"Call upon whomever you want. You and he can die together. Perhaps holding hands." I was surprised at my own self. I guess this is what happens when you've been hurt so much. You become numb. You become cold hearted.

"I have more." Willow said. *Ohm this bitch is bold.* It really amazed me. I sat quiet waiting for the remainder of the shenanigans to play out.

"She takes no husband. She's unfit to lead. She loves three different men. Her virtue is not intact. She's tainted."

Now everyone gasped. Father shouted at her after hearing her false allegations. "It's true. Tell everyone Katianna. Tell everyone how you've kissed all three me. Him, him, and him." She pointed at Thomas, then Lee, then T-B-N. My heart began to fold in my chest. For the first time she was right about something. I felt shame.

I felt the scowls in all three of their faces as they were pointed out. Lee stood up to speak. "You're a fool, watch your tongue...." She cut him off. "Or what. You'll cut it out of my mouth like you threatened me by the stone walls." Lees eyebrows furrowed at her advance.

"I did no such thing."

"Nonsense." Mr. Punic slammed his hand to the desk. "What evidence do you have of your accusations.?"

"I've heard it first-hand. Seen things with my own eyes. I shapeshifted as Victoria, her lady maiden. She is no virgin."

Everyone's eyes laid on my naked. Bare, for all to see. At least that's how I felt. They all wanted answers. If being put on the spot was a person, then hi, it's me. I rose from my chair. Wishing I could be that frightened little girl I was just months ago. Instead, I must face vexatious ugly truths. I sucked in a deep breath.

"Her allegations of my mother's death being related to my powers is false. There is no truth to that. I am powerfully gifted. Nothing more. The accusation of my virtue is also a lie. I am pleased to inform everyone about MY body. My virginity is intact. But she was right about one thing she said." I paused watching everybody fixated on me.

If holding your breath was a person. Then it is everyone here. "I did kiss three men. I have built bonds with three different men. I find no wrongdoing in that. How am I to find a husband if I don't get to know people."

"Bullshit." She shouted. "Then tell us. Whose it gonna be."

My heart won't let me look at either of them. As I'm sure they are all looking at me. Who the hell is she to come in my Court after attempting to take my life and turn everything around on me. "Are you wed Willow?"

"Of course, I am. I wed the same week I converted. Unlike you, I take my reign seriously."

"And do you love your new husband?. Congratulations by the way. Maybe I'll give him your head in a box as a gift."

"You're evil. You bitch."

"No, you're evil bitch. Shapeshifting into people's bodies to get close to me. You're sick. Now answer the question. I'm getting tired."

"Love doesn't matter. Maybe one day I......I mean I like him and were getting to know each other."

"Excatly. And that is the difference between you and I dear. You do as your told. SOOO typical you are. I.DO.AS. I. PLEASE." The room volleyed between her and I. No one interrupted. No one even so much as breathed too heavily.

"You are here because you tried to kill me. You used a man I......" I stopped in my tracks. Realizing what I was about to say. "You used a dear friend of mines to get close to me. Somehow to save your own ass you dug up pointless dirt."

"Still can't choose can you." She laughed.

"You really think I answer to you. Silly girl. I'm done with this. Take her back to the hole until David is interrogated. I have nothing to hide. And by the way, my powers are much greater than yours because of the challenge I had to pass to get them. Whereas you and all the other Villages convert simply off being chosen. There's no meaning behind that. You didn't train like I, you didn't sweat, hurt, bleed, cry, lose sleep, you didn't go through shit, and you don't know shit…stupid."

"Fine. If you won't then I will. She's more in love with……" I froze her mouth shut immediately. My heart raced. Not because I was afraid of what she would say, but because she talked too damn much. I don't care what she's seen or heard. No one knows my heart better than my soul.

Forget about her weird sudden interest in my love life. I was more upset with the way she spoke about my mother.

How dare she accuse her of selling her own life just so that I could have extra powers. None of it made sense. There was only one person who could make sense of it all. And he was already awaiting trial for his own bullshit.

I wonder what part he plays in this. I won't know until tonight. Until then I have my vivid imagination of me taking both their heads myself.

As the room cleared out, I heard Lee asking Jackson, the former leader of white, where his man was. Something about having left him behind in White because he was sick, but apparently, he never returned.

The conversation got heated and a woman from White grabbed Lee by his arm. She wrapped her arms around him tight. Practically jumping on him. I heard him call her Lily.

Who the fuck is Lily. I dismissed Parliament and assured them there were to be a council meeting held at first light. My eyes would not pry away from Lee and this strange woman.

"I've missed you. When I heard there was a chance to come to Blue for a hearing, I traded everything I had for a spot on the ten. I knew you weren't from White. I suppose I always knew. When I asked around about you after you disappeared. A kitchen boy told me you were from blue and was there to find some missing girl." They had no idea I was standing behind them. "Brennon, do you miss me?" She called him Brennon. It's the weirdest thing. Then again, weird is the new normal.

When he realized I was standing right behind them, his heart gulped in his throat. His eyes begged me to believe there was more to the story. And I, sad to say, was hurt. Maybe I had no right to be, but I am. I channeled a power I never used before. It was mind reading. I guess it channeled when I felt so badly the need to get inside his head.

"Fuck, fuck, fuck. Shit. Got dammit." He thought. I stood there. He stood there. I looked. He looked. The poor Lily girl was staring at the both of us in confusion. For she does not know her fate.

"Who's your friend Brennon?" She leaned and kissed him on the cheek. Standing next to him like they were a real couple, and I was the one who was on the outside looking in.

"Friend....I..." He cut me off.

"She is Lady Katianna, leader of Blue."

"Oh, ok. Hi."

My eyes might as well had jumped out its sockets and put her to death. As hard as I was rolling them.

"Yeah, who's your friend Brennon?" I think he understood my sarcasm. Better than she did, because she responded for him. "Hi, I'm Lily from White. Brennon's Lady and future Wife." My eyebrows furrowed at her ridiculous beliefs. *What in the hell does he have this poor girl believing.* She extended her hand for a shake. I bumped them both as I brushed past.

The last thing I wanted was to cause a scene and turn that poor girl into dust.

Besides I had too much to think about then to be jealous over whatever it was that was happening with Lee, I mean Brennon apparently. When he didn't chase after me, in a desperate attempt to explain, I felt burned. Tears held its place in ducts.

****

TWENTY-SEVEN

KATIANNA

It's all too much for me to handle. I have no help. I feel defeated as I lay in my bed. Lord knows how tonight's gonna go after I add in my demands on top of all the chaotic messes that are already in place.

Maybe, just maybe, I should have stepped down of my duties. At least I had something to look forward too. My little brothers arrive tomorrow morning. I've missed them so much.

I had a few visitors at my Chambers. Father gave me his opinion on how I should move forward.

The real Victoria came, and I had to tell her that her body was being used as a hostess for a shapeshifter.

She didn't seem surprised at all. In fact, she explained to me how weird she'd been feeling. How she didn't feel like herself lately. She too, gave me some valid points.

The people I really need, aren't here. I thought about what my mother would do.

If I'm being honest, I know for certain that this situation wouldn't be playing out this long. Everyone would have been dead a long time ago.

Death brings revenge. Revenge brings war. The last thing I want is to wage war. My people have suffered enough as is.

I would never forgive myself if more blood spilled on the count of me. However, I also can't appear to be weak.

If I simply let Willow off the hook, that would make me vulnerable. People are going to see me and see a target. The guards knocked. "Enter." I called out.

They gave me word that Thomas wanted to speak with me. He waited in my office. Which was once mother's green room.

I've kept some things the way it was. I wasn't a big, surround myself with flowers, the way she was.

When I arrived, he was leaning against the window frame. Facing me once I presented. "Please. Sit with me."

"Is everything alright Thomas?"

"Everything is fine. I am more worried about you. I don't need you to worry about me."

"I'm well. I'm not fazed by her ridiculous accusations." I leaned back in the chair grabbing a cup of fresh tea. Which was always replaced every hour.

I looked at the tea before I put my lips to it, setting it back down as I inspected it.

I found nothing odd other than my gut feeling., and with all this poising going on. I no longer trusted anything to eat or drink unless I saw it prepared myself. Mother had a taster. I'll be sure to have one as well.

"I'm not them Katianna. You don't have to be strong for me. I know you. The real you. Tell me how you feel."

I sighed running my fingers through my hair. I sunk my shoulders. "I feel overwhelmed. I feel like a crazy person. I feel like I'm not ready. I feel like I want my mother back. I feel……I feel uncertain." I sat there with my eyes closed.

"Look at me." I looked at him. "It's ok to feel all of those things. Your life changed literally overnight. That's 'enough to drive anybody mad. Lead with your heart. Do what you deem best. You are the strongest woman I know. Don't overthink it. Close your eyes like you always do, and the answers will find its way to your heart."

I knew he was right. I stayed back awhile after he left. With my eyes closed.

Memories worked their way to my vision. I was channeling without channeling. I seen war. I see all Villages in the battlefield just outside Blues gates.

This wasn't a memory. It's a prophet. My premonitions were clear. There will be war. I don't know when, how, or why, but it's coming, and soon. I have the upper hand knowing this. My men, and my people will be ready.

"Victoria." I called out for her when I reached my Chambers.

"Yes, my lady."

"Send for my father, and for all the members on parliament to meet me in the war room. NOW."

The first thing I did was alarm them of my visions. I ordered them to prepare. I ordered my brothers to be halted and sent back to safety.

No one questioned my visions. They saw it in my demeanor that I was serious, and this was real. Now I must go give speech to the people. I'll do it after tonight's deliberation with David.

I rounded up Stella and rode off to alarm all those I could before the hearing. Mostly guards, my top skillful fighters, and those who were skillful to precision with their weapons.

My bowmen's and swordsman especially. I rather have them on alert then not at all.

The regular Villagers will be prepped later. I doubled up security at the flood gates and all entrances and exits.

I wanted White out our hear before they get wind of what we're doing.

Last thing I need is for them to have a heads up. They are no ally of ours. In fact, in my vision, they're the ones that led.

The Black Knight(T-B-N) rode up beside me and Stella on his horse. I alarmed him of what's happened. He immediately sent word to his Village. They were to arrive by first light. We'll house them for as long as we needed to.

"James." I called to him before he could ride off. I had to know. "Why?"

"Why…. why what?"

"Why are you helping me when I didn't…. you know."

"Black will always be your ally. I told you that no matter what. Black is in debt to your mother. She saved us years ago. Besides whether you fell for me or not. I still feel for you." He winked and rode off.

I was amazed at his kindness. I was even more amazed to learn that my mother did something amazing for others. I had no idea she helped Black.

I wondered in which way exactly. Just another question I needed answers to.

David stood tall at the hearing. Willow was brought back in. They looked at each other discerningly. Like they won something. The smirk on her face gave it away.

"David you were called here as a witness. This is not the hearing for your disloyal acts against Mary-Ann, my mother, who you're accused of murdering. That is a separate issue. So, stick to why you're here."

"Then why am I here.?"

"Shut Up. You speak only when spoken to." Something about hearing his nasty voice irritated me.

"This……" I laughed sarcastically as I pointed to Willow. "This might as well be a commoner has implicated you as a witness to some very disturbing lies. She's said you play a hand in knowing my powers were given to me under false pretenses, she said my mother sold her soul so that I can be powerfully gifted. So please tell us what you know…. now you speak."

He cleared his throat before saying. "What I know is that your bloodline decent from witches. Years ago, the women of your family were first born witches. Your mother included, and now you. It's why your powerfully gifted. Your mother will have done anything for you. She loved you more than anyone, but sell her soul to earn you extra powers, she did not." Willow screamed at him to tell the truth.

"You're lying to save yourself. Tell them. Tell them what you told me in the hole."

"I told you about her having witch in her blood. Yes, that I did say. I admit that. Thanks for keeping that secret like you promised me you would. I would never speak of a dear friend that way. I would never say she sold her soul, that was your assumption. Not mines."

"She's still a witch."

"Guards take her away. I will render judgment at first light."

Willow kicked and screamed all the way out the door. She channeled her powers shapeshifting to different people, but it didn't work.

Her body needed to be completely free in order to fully inhabit another's body as a hostess. She only had half her powers.

"Before we are dismissed, I will say this. The rule about leaders needing to wed to be able to rule, veto. I will do no such thing. My father has already spoken with members from The Vatican and the priest himself. They send us their blessings. You can check if you want. This. Is. My. Time. My reign. My rules. Anyone with a problem can see me. I will marry when I want, who I want, how I want, and where I want."

Jackson shouted and laughed. "Pathetic. This Village is weak. A joke. Who are you to change the rules. Rules are rules for a reason. If you don't let my daughter go, there will be more than an attempt on your life."

"Is that so?" I locked eyes on him. I channeled earth manipulation to constrict his body. Sending him off his feet and thrown against the wall high up in the air.

Everyone watched in horror. I no longer cared what people thought. If I am to be labeled a witch, then I sure as hell am going to enjoy being one.

I don't care how or why I'm powerfully gifted. I earned it, I have it, and plan on accepting and using it to the best of my abilities. I'm sick of people testing me.

Now I see why my mother was the way she was. You have to be this way. I let him down when I saw his breath fading and his face turning blue. "Now go run tell that. Get you and the other nine and get the hell out of my home. She has committed a crime and is now my prisoner. Shall I choose execution. No worries I'll let you and her mother say goodbye. I'm not a monster, just a witch." Eyes scolded me, especially Lilys. She looked at me like if she could kill me, she would.

They all looked at me like that. Oh well, tomorrows another day.

Attention drew from me to a dingy frail looking woman entering the hearing. She walked like she could barely walk. She breathed like she could barely breath. She looked half dead.

"Come no further. Who are you?" Her face was in ruins. She looked scary. Maybe she was the monster from the woods. Maybe she was the reason behind countless children reporting of having nightmares and sightings of a strange woman.

"I'm Gracey. David's wife." The attention turned from me, to her, to him. I've heard about her plenty of time. I've only ever caught glimpse.

"If you are here to save your husband, don't bother. It will do him more harm than good."

"I'm here to relieve him in place of me. I killed Mary-Ann. It was me, he had nothing to do with it."

"Gracey stop it." David yelled to his wife. "Go back to our Chambers."

"No. It's true. I switched the berries with poisoned ones. I added poison to your potion of medicine."

"Why. Why would you do that?" he pleaded.

"Because I was jealous. You think I couldn't see that you were in love with her. The way you looked at her." She snarled. "I know that look. The way you talked about her. She was all you ever talked about. You spent more time with her than me. You called her name when we made love. And I hated her for it. But I love you still. Love you enough that I cannot watch you killed for my crimes."

The fire burned in me. I knew she was telling the truth. My powers told me so.

So did the way David looked at her in complete oblivion. My entire body was undulating. I tried to control it. I tried to breath.

Fire inflamed my being. People scattered. Some hid wherever they could. Before I knew it, Gracey was ash.

Nothing more than a pile of dust. David received third degree burns on his arms in his attempt to save his wife. He was on his knees at her pile of ash. Crying out to her.

"Take him to the infirmary to be treated for his wounds. Then he can go. He's to be exiled."

"You bitch." He lunged, but I froze him.

"Listen and listen good. Your wife killed my mother. A Village leader out of jealousy. You're lucky you're still breathing." The guards took him away. Out the corner of my eyes I seen a wolf. I smiled inside knowing exactly what it was.

"Let's go. We must go. This Village is nuts You have fires, wolves, death. We'll come back for her." Mia said to her twin as the two ran off cowardly.

"Brennon, can I stay with you?" Lily pleaded. He said nothing. All he did was look at me. I read his mind. "Damn I want nothing more than to take her right here, right now. If only she knew how sexy she was." I smirked.

Breaking our gaze to one another. Even after all this. Even after he had a girl pulling at his arm begging him to stay, he thought of being with me. It turned me on.

I escaped to the memory of him touching me in the kitchen. He walked towards me pushing Lilys arm off his shoulder.

"You look flushed. Your cheeks are red, are you ok?" No,

I'm not ok Lee, I just read your mind. If only you knew.

"I'm fine. I just channeled fire." I lied. "Why do you care?"

Lee explained to me his whole ordeal with the Lily girl. He told me it was all a ploy to get information. I believed him. It made my decision no easier.

I may be relieved of my duty to wed, but that didn't mean I didn't want to love and share my life with someone. I'm more confused than ever before.

Perhaps The Mother was right all along. I should have wed by her force. That way, at least I'd be able to cower behind my vexatious truth.

Lee walked me to my Chambers, and I had to endure all his intrusive thoughts along the way. How he wanted to taste my lips. Both lips. How he wanted to kill any other man if I chose them. It was as endearing as it was sick. Guards rushed us at the doors.

"My lady. We just received word of an army headed our way. Their south of the border. They're coming for us."

Panic took over as I tried to wrap my head around how quickly my visions were coming true.

I didn't think it would be happening this fast. We won't be aided by our allies in time. Thus, leaving us less equipped.

I must send an army of men ahead to take out as much people as they can to stop them from attacking our borders. Lee was already in route the moment he heard the news.

I sounded the alarm for emergency battle. Villagers knew to gather at the rally point.

"My people. We have just received word of an army headed our way. I will send a group of warriors ahead to try and stop what we could. Send all the children to the bunker. We need all hands-on deck. Including women strong enough to fight. If you're weak or too old, head to the bunker with the children. Everyone else prepare for war. I'm told they'll reach us by nightfall."

People scattered. Panicked. Crying. Praying. It was catastrophic.

A lot of them already lost their loved ones. Now I was asking them to go through yet another round of losses. But not if my powers could help.

T-B-N sent word ahead to his Village to send men along with Blue. He too volunteered to go ahead, and I needed him too. He's certainly the best swordsman I know.

"I won't ask you to fight." I frantically told Thomas. "But my people are in danger." He grabbed my hands.
"Take a deep breath."
"I'm scared Thomas. What if.."
"Stop. I will be at your side. Nothing is going to happen to you."
'It's not me I'm scared for. It's my people."
"Then I will ride ahead and fight front line to make sure nothing happens to them either."
"I don't deserve you." I kissed his cheek.
"You deserve all of me." He kissed my cheek in return.

My Village was in shambles. Disarrayed. And there was nothing I could do about it. Except watch it all unfold. As time wind down. We waited.

Men were ready to ride off. I looked for Lee. My heart was scared for them all, but I had to see Lee.

In case I never get to see him again. I'd feel awful if I never got to say goodbye like how I didn't get to do so with Stacey.

Regardless of my heart for another, Lee was a part of my original crew. We're still friends.

Moving through the crowd and shifting my way through horses. I spotted Lee.

"Lee." I called for his attention. He turned his horse around. "Be careful please. Come back to me."

He gazed down at me with lust lingering in his beautiful eyes. "Always."

"Where is your armor, is that all you are wearing." I pulled at his vest. Wondering where his shield was.

"Your heart is the only armor I'll ever need, and I'll wear it proudly until the day I die, and even after that, because I'll choose you again, and again, and again, in any lifetime, in every realm. I'll find you. Because I am yours. I love you more than love."

Tears were threatening to make an appearance. I felt his words in my stomach. I knew he meant every word of it.

"Don't…..don't say stuff like that to me. That's not fair." I held his gaze. "Come back to me."

"Give me a reason worth fighting to come back for." He lifted his helmet.

"Come back, and you'll find that reason waiting." I grabbed his hand. He smiled at me. His hand slipped slowly as his horse trotted away.

I had to give him hope. I'd give all of them hope if it meant they'd fight a little harder. T-B-N rode up shortly after. "Half my men were sent ahead to meet us; the other half were sent here to aid you. Please stay alive. I haven't shown you the best parts of me yet." He winked and rode off.

There was one more face I needed to see. Only I didn't see Thomas at all. I found my horse and mounted on her so I can ride out and see if I could find him.

There was no way I'd let him leave without saying something. I found him far off the flood gates.

He was mounted on his horse Grey. Stella stopped next to Grey. I dismounted and tied her to the willow. Thomas dismounted tying Grey as well.

"Why are you over here and not with the others."

"I take no pleasure in watching you say goodbye to other men. I take no pleasure in being where I don't fit in. I will fight for you. In fact, I'm honored to do so. Once it's over. I was thinking I'd rebuild Grey Village from scratch. Find whomever I could to join me. Outsiders perhaps. Give people with no home, a home. I'd finally belong somewhere to someone. I'd finally matter."

"You matter Thomas. You matter to me. Look at me." He looked at me with those grey eyes. Grey looked good on him. His horse, his Village, his armor. "You matter. You have a home here in Blue. You know that don't you."

"I do, but you know what I'm saying. It's not the same. I admire you. I admire your home. But that's what it is. Your home, not mine. I'm not exactly a fall in line kind of guy. I'm a leader. Always have been. I need my own home, Katianna. But I promise you Grey, whenever I rebuild, will be your number one Ally. I will always run for you."

"I see. I suppose I do understand. I can't deny that it makes me sad. I also can't deny the mess I've put you in. You were fine before you met me, but I wouldn't trade it for the world. I'll cherish what we had in the woods forever."

He pulled something from his rucksack. "Close your eyes and open your hands" I closed my eyes. He placed some sort of object in my palms. "Feel."

My eyes were still closed but he circled around me. "Feel." He whispered in my ear. "What do you feel." I breathed deep in and out. In and out.

"I feel you. I feel your wolf. I feel my spirit." I continued tracing whatever he placed in my hands. It felt like one of his toys. I mean, one of his wooden sculptures. "Good, open your eyes."

I looked down at a wooden sculpture. It was a carving of a wolf mixed with a lioness. It was us.

He once referred to me as a lioness. He always said it was my spirit animal.

The sculpture told me more with me eyes closed than it did with them open. It was beautiful. It was sculpted to precision. I can tell he took his time on this piece. I was at a loss for words. Literally.

"Don't you go forgetting about me."

"Never. My wolf boy."

"You better not. My witch girl." We both laughed.

"They look ready to ride off. I must go. I'll see you again."

"Thomas….wait." I grabbed him before he mounted. The look in his eyes paralyzed me.

Why is he the only man who doesn't beg me to choose him. Why is he the only man my heart skips beats for.

He pulled me into him. Why is he the only man I fold for. The way my mother did for my father. Taking charge of what he knew I desperately wanted.

I didn't have to say it. He held the back of my head inserting his tongue in my mouth. Sparks flew inside of me channeling electric currents through waves in my body. "It's you. I choose you. I want you. I. Need. You. Thomas. I'm in love with you." Tears rolled down my face in defeat as he held me in his arms.

It all made sense now. I understand why it never worked with no one else. Because it wasn't supposed to. Because of him. *Got damn you Thomas.*

"Are you fucking serious." He said grabbing my face in his hands. "Do you know how long I've waited for you to feel that. To hear you say that. My love. I'm in love with you too." He kissed me again.

We nearly jumped each other's bones right there against the Willow tree.

"Come Home my love. We'll build Grey together. We will make it home together. Just come home." I had no idea what I was saying.

He was Grey. I am Blue, and there's no way I was gonna leave my Village. But there was also no way I will live without him.

"I promise." He spoke.

"You promise."

"I promise." We kissed once more before he rode off. I took off soon after to gear up. I planned on fighting shall it come to it.

TWENTY-EIGHT

KATIANNA

The Village was the quietest I've ever heard it. Everyone was so focused concentrating on any sign of battle.

The men T-B-N sent arrived just moments ago. I was glad to have his men by our side. Their animals in human form.

Nothing but cold wind swept through the Village. Suddenly arrows were descending from the sky. "Shield." I screamed and froze whatever arrows I could. War began.

Some arrows made it through before I froze. Resulting in the death of some ladies and soldiers.

I grew angry, but it was hard to channel fire when the enemies were behind the walls. I nodded the guards to open the flood gates.

If we had any chance to attack, we had to do so now. I ordered the bowmen to release their arrows up and over the gates.

I could hear the defeat of fallen men from the arrows we sent. I could literally hear life leave their bodies.

When the gates were fully lifted. Thousands of men flooded our grounds. I channeled fire burning hundreds. I threw electric shocks killing instantly.

I didn't bother using my free. That was only good for a one-on-one kind of thing.

I got knocked of Stella as she fell due to being pierced with a sword. My poor Stella wept at me. The soul was fading out of her eyes.

I placed my hand on her and channeled fire. Putting her out her misery I burned her to ash. Along with the persons whose sword pierced her.

I was now on foot. It was like a jungle. Swords swung everywhere. Blood spilled everywhere. So much blood spilled that the grounds were slick with it. I thought about if the ones we sent ahead were ok.

During my trance I got glazed with a sword. I threw my daggers piercing the neck of the man who grazed me.

His limp dropped instantly. I retreated my daggers and wiped his blood off. Slicking it to the floor.

I jumped over bodies throwing daggers at whoever I could. I channeled earth manipulation breaking the ground we stood on. Separating Villages by the leaders I saw.

White was not in attendance because their leader is busy trapped in the black hole. However, I see some of their people fighting alongside Brown. I threw fire, I threw shocks, I threw the ocean at these motherfuckers.

When I threw ocean. A whole section depleted. There was magic everywhere as all Leaders channeled their powers.

Why'd they hate me so much. I have no clue. But hating me was the wrong thing to do. I saw a dagger coming straight at my head. I ducked.

When I looked to right of me. The man who threw the dagger was shot with a bow. I traced my sight back to whom threw the fatal shot at him. I saw David.

His arm was wrapped from his burn injury, but he was still on. Bow and arrow. He clearly escaped the infirmary.

He nodded his head for me to get my head back in the game. I drew sword face to face with a woman.

She was a woman but was built like a man. "You think your some kind of warrior princess. Why don't you fight me one on one, leave your powers home."

We rocked back and forth like we were characters of Street Fighter. "I don't need powers to kill you. I'll do that with my bare hands." She laughed as she charged at me.

I lost my footing as she took me down from my ankles. We were tussling on the floor. I had to kill this big bitch, and quick.

My people still needed me. I threw punches, she threw harder ones. I'm sure I have cracked rib. I don't know how I'm going to win without my powers.

I fought with everything I had in me to be released from her grip.

Her hands were tightening around my neck. Squeezing like a snake do to it's prey. I was losing breath.

Too weak to even channel a power. I stupidly let her in my head. I should have never agreed to fighting without powers. Now here I am, fading.

I can see darkness when I closed my eyes. Suddenly her grip released, and I could breathe again.

When I sucked in air. Her head was ripped off her shoulders, and a big ass grey wolf looked me in my eyes. Relief came to me as I realized they were back.

Either that or he projected his wolf ahead. I still wasn't sure of the attributes his wolf came with. His wolf fought alongside me.

He was ripping off limbs and heads, and I was spitting fire and throwing dagger.

I wrapped bunches of people with the vines from the ground holding them against the willows until I could get to them to kill them one by one.

Darkness enveloped the earth. It was already dark from night. But this was different.

Everything turned pitch black. No one could see their own hand before them. I can feel Wolf on my legs. I reached my hand down to pet him.

Although I didn't have to reach down far.

Darkness faded to brightness. Everyone lifted their arm to cover their eyes. The brightness was too bright. I didn't see Thomas, Lee, or T-B-N.

Which told me Thomas projected. I screamed in the middle of this all. I screamed and screamed and screamed.

The words that flew out of my mouth was not my own. It felt like something took over my body.

"STOP THIS MADNESS." I screamed as I looked to everyone. "Look all around you. Senseless lives lost. Why must me continue this madness. Can anybody even tell me what we're at war for besides jealousy, hatred, and mis communication." No one answered.

For some reason I feel like I can get through to these people. "So what, one Village has more than another. That is why we trade. So what, one Village differs from another, that's what makes us, us. We are all unique. I propose a mutual grounding. I propose a new era. I propose new treaties. We are living in the new age. It's a new Dawn everyone. Who said we had to follow traditional rules. Those rules were made centuries ago. Life has changed. You have changed. I have changed. WE......We are changed. Don't you people get it. Why live in blood when we can have peace. The Gods have spoken to me. That was the reason for the Darkness. They are livid with the way we carry on hating each other. They are threatening to wipe the world out completely. If you don't believe me, then stay, lets fight." I shook my head up and down. "I assure you; no one will win here. We should be teaching and raising our children and working to support our families. Now, we can go on, or we can call a truce and hold meeting to discuss issues like adults. I promise you all. I'm highly favor and powerfully gifted. You will not win against me. So, what's it gonna be. Brown?" I questioned them first.

Their leader stepped out front center. "We keep getting the shit end of the stick. Your mother broke our treaty many times. Our people are suffering. We need help."

"Come here. Come stand with me." He came to my side. "I am not my mother. I don't rule like my mother. We will help you." I blinked my eyes up and down to him. I can feel the settling in his demeanor.

"Anyone else?" Leaders and their peoples came forth one by one with their complaints and demands. I smiled. It was a war that turned into something more. Something more innovative.

I promised to hold personal meetings with each Village one by one. Starting tomorrow. I summoned everyone to go home.

When the crowd depleted. I saw Thomas. Standing behind a crowd of Vikings. His face brought an immediate smile to mines. I jumped in his arms.

Inspecting the gash, he had on his face. He inspected my neck and my rib cage when I squirmed as he hugged me back.

"So, my Witch girl can persuade a whole army of people to back down and start a new world order. "

"I guess I had some motivation." I kissed him. I looked at him and he knew exactly what the look was.

"Your father was injured on the front lines. He's in infirmary." I broke away immediately and ran to my father's side.

I'd be damned if I lose another parent. He was pierced through one of his lungs. Tears flooded my eyes, watching him gasp for breath. "Will he be ok Doctor?"

"He will live. It will be an extensive recovery, but he will make it. He's getting sutured in a few minutes. We had to open him up to stop the bleeding."

"Thank You Doctor." I hugged him. "Please take care of my father. Spare no expense. Whatever he needs."

"Of course." Doctor Amelie assured me.

Thomas was right outside the infirmary. He scooped me in his arms and alerted the doctor that once he was finished with my father.

He was to come to my Chambers to tend to me next. I was too weak to even fight against it. My ribs needed repair.

He carried me all the way to my Chambers. He layed me down and attempted to walk away.

"The Doctor will come. Let him in and let him see you. You have a broken rib. Until then. Sleep."

I peeled my eyes open. "Are you always this bossy?"

He smiled at me. "It's the wolf in me." I tried to laugh but the pain in my sides stumped me as I grabbed myself.

"Careful, careful." He removed my hand from my wound. Inspecting it once more.

"Thomas. Where is Lee and James?"

"They are both fine. I see why you favored each of them. They're both stand up men. Lee was injured, but not severely. I had to save him from being killed."

"Did you."

"I did. I have no reason to let a man die who loves the one I love. He cares for you."

"I know, but I am yours."

"I know."

I love him even more for the kind man that he is. He could have easily let Lee die. Instead, he spared his life, and I know he did it for me.

Lee will be hurt when he finds out I chose to be with Thomas, but at least he's alive. For now.

There's no telling where his anger will lead him. He once said in his head that he'd kill any man I chose, and if he thinks he can kill Thomas. Then, he has another thing coming.

He left out and came back with a bucket of water and a cloth. He wet it and rung it out and cleaned my face first.

He then soft cleaned the area where my ribs were broken. It was a nasty looking wound. It was purple and black. It reminded me of how human I was despite all the powers I have.

"Do you need anything, are you hungry or thirsty. You should eat something."

"Water." He returned moments later with water, and lifted my head so I could drink. Suddenly I was a little girl and needed him to feed me water even though I didn't. Sitting up hurted like a bitch but it was not, not manageable.

"Stay with me." I held his gaze and watched as he climbed in my bed.

We layed facing each other on our sides. Of course, I laid on my left side due to injury on my right. "Tell me a story."

"Yup, a story, any story."

"Are you asking I tell you a bedtime story?" His eyebrows furrowed.

"Please."

"An old man traveled with a compass. He said he'd find his way to the moon. He stopped at each town within his country, telling everyone of his journey, asking everyone for their help. They all laughed at him. He kept chugging along until he made a stop at a Cottage he spotted. Inside that Cottage housed three small children. Ruby, Magda, and Charles. They told him their parents left them and that they had been alone for days. The man felt sorry for them and gave them the last of his food…...."

****

"How long have I been asleep?"

"Long enough that you missed the doctor and a very angry Lee, and then a very annoying James. Oh, and a very worried father." I tried to jump up at the mentioning of my father, but my injuries clearly got the best of me.

"Your father is fine. He's resting in his chambers. The doctor will be back soon. I asked him to let you rest awhile longer. You looked so peaceful."

TWENTY-NINE

KATIANNA

Weeks passed since the war. My father is fully healed. I am fully healed. Peace smells good in the air.

Lee didn't take it too well about my being with Thomas. I gave him space. I didn't see him for two weeks when he first found out.

It broke my heart to break his heart, but I'm doing whatever makes me happy. It was always a stupid rule.

Whoever said one must be miserable to reign. I have my cake, and I'm going to eat it too.

There were a few discrepancies to some of the new rules I placed in panel. Not all my new rules were accepted, but the ones that mattered the most, did.

A leader, shall it be a male or female does not have to be wed to rule.

Over time I met with each Village leader and the members of their panel to go over new treaties.

Each had their own valid points. I did the best I could without draining all the resources from my own Village.

Allison is set to come next month on her eighteenth birthday. It was the only reason Lee broke the silence between us.

He needed my permission and my letter of recommendation to send for her. Of course, I did. She didn't live in any of the Villages. She lived halfway across the world in Demark with her aunt, her uncle and cousins.

The day Lee did speak to me about it, he kept it short. I tried to ask him how he was doing, but he ignored any questions that were personal. T-B-N, retreated to his Village.

He had a hard time accepting my decision too, but he respected me. He told me one day he'll change my mind. Black Village remains our strongest alliance.

As for Thomas, he nursed me back to health. He went back to the woods but showed up every day just to have supper with me.

We've done nothing but kiss and touch, and it's driving me crazy. He still has his big plans of rebuilding Grey Village.

I fully support him and have sent multiple resources to aid him in his journey. As his journey is now my journey.

Noah and Joe. Jr are back home for now. Father keeps watch on them, and they have many guards and nannies.

They both have gotten so big in the matter of a short time they were away.

My mother was finally layed to rest two days after the war. The ceremony was beautiful. I fell into another slump about it.

Held up in my room and cried for days. Thomas was there every second besides me.

I've learned so much more about my powers. Thomas has done well teaching me how to control it. I try not to use them if I don't have to.

There are days, I've had to. I have two more ladies now. So, three altogether, I didn't have the heart to let Victoria go.

It wasn't her fault she got tricked. I now have her, Layla, and Rebecca. Hopefully Allison when she comes.

Thomas has a special dinner planned for us tonight. The ladies are helping me ready.

"Sooo, do you think he'll pop the question?" Layla asked. Victoria and I smiled to each other. She was brushing my hair like she always did. No one could ever take her spot. It was such a simple thing, but it was our thing.

"Pop the question. He hasn't even popped her cherry." Rebecca countered. We all laughed.

Rebecca was the silly one of us all. I like that about her. When we are all bickering, she always does things to get us all talking again.

She was like the fun big sister. Victoria remained the quiet-sweet one. Layla and I, we were the wild ones.

We bickered more than the others. She always teased me about still being a virgin, even though she was one herself. It felt good having girlies around me.

None of them will ever amount to Stacey, but it still felt good.

"Remind us, why haven't you taken that fine Thomas down yet? You set a rule about not having to be wed. So why are you holding out?"

"I'm still a respectable lady Layla. I still believe in virtue." She snarled shaking her head in a silly way to mock me. She loved doing impersonations of me.

"Well, if you're not using him, pass him to me." I rose from my chair and held my dagger to her neck.

"Kati, chill out, she's just kidding." Rebecca said.

"Sorry." I realized my anger didn't fit the mold.

"Geesh Kati, you'll kill over him. You're in love girl." They all laughed. I didn't find it amusing.

I will kill over him. I'll kill over Lee to, and I don't even have any rights too.

Just days ago, I heard of him becoming friendly with one of the ladies. It was told to me that they kissed and made love.

That is what said lady told her friend, who is friends, with my friend Jerrica. Jerrica was not one of my maidens, because she's highly ranked with title.

Her parents are wealthy, and she has enough monies in her dowry, that she doesn't need title in Court.

We were always friends. Our friendship kicked up more when she started spilling secrets to me. A commoner girl named Judy.

Victoria had to talk me out of turning her to ash and dust. I still cared for Lee, as a friend. I'm still very much protective of him.

Thomas and I have had many disagreements about it. He even threatened our relationship if I didn't give Lee up completely.

Each time I told him I did, and that Lee was just a friend, and he will always be just a friend. Truth be told, I do still feel something for Lee, and I think I always will. You can't just erase years of history.

Honestly, there were moments where I questioned my decision.

I wondered if chose Thomas because he helped me so much, and because I felt him slipping away when he said he was going to build his own Village back up.

Which I thought I could persuade him to do otherwise once I chose him. He has this big plan that we will either merge our Villages, or we will lead separately and still be together.

I honestly don't see how it could happen. I snapped back to reality.

"I'm truly sorry Layla. I've been on edge lately.

"It's ok you whore." She bumped my hip with hers. It was something we did. Along with calling each other names. Whores, sluts, and all kinds of bitches. We understood, only we could talk to each other that way, and it was only to be done amongst each other.

"Guys, I really hope he makes a move tonight." I said as I stared in the mirror.

"Do you feel like you're ready?" Victoria asked.

"I know how I feel when I'm with him. So, yes. I'm ready."

"Awwwwww." Layla and Rebecca synchronized.

****

He sent for me when he arrived. We rode out on his horse. It was nice. Body to body nice.

My hair whipped in the wind. His body felt so masculine with my arms wrapped around him. My guards had to be stationed to me at all times.

They rode a few feet away to give us privacy. The further we went into the woods, the more I was aware of where we were going.

He helped me down from his horse and took my hand in his. "Back to the beginning?" I asked. It was his Cottage.

"Yes. Back to the beginning."

It looked so different from when I was here last. It was cleaner. It had more furniture. It was brighter.

The room that was once locked when I first came here was filled with sculptures. He left me inspect every room while he started a fire in the pit.

There was a dinner display on the logs he used for table. That he probably carved and made himself. "You're quite the handyman."

He smiled. "Why, yes." He poured wine and handed me a glass.

"Hi, I'm Thomas, do you always hit yourself on your head and talk to yourself."

"Ohhh. I see what you're doing." I got into character. "Are you always an ass. Are you the monster in the woods."

"Well. I don't know. Either you want my help or not."

"Not." I got up pretending like I was going to leave the way I did when we first me.

He pulled me back into him, so that I was now cradling his lap. He trailed his fingers down my arm, and down my stomach, then down my thighs. "Beautiful."

He motioned his face up so that I would perceive him for wanting to kiss. I leaned down to allow his access.

I playfully pulled back when his lips almost touched mines, but he grabbed the back of my neck forcing me to kiss him. I draped my legs over him.

Fully seated in his lap now. One leg over each side. Electric rose inside me as I became excited.

It was magical. Kissing him with the sound of fire burning wood. "I could have sparked that for you, you know." I nodded my head towards the fire.

We both laughed. He slipped his tongue right back into my mouth. He was such a gentleman. Never taking it further than where I wanted it to go.

I placed his hands on my ass. He needed no more permission as he grabbed my ass pushing my body further into him.

Working his tongue on my neck, down to the center of my collar bone. I wanted more. I moaned softly from his tongue, and from every touch he touched. "I need to ask you something?" He picked me up in his arms.

My pussy throbbed and leaked with slickness. I didn't care what the question was. I wanted him to make love to me. I'd agree to anything right about now. He carried me to the room in the back, that now had a full bed. The room I once occupied as my own.

"Do you love me more than him? Will you marry me?" He looked me deeply in my eyes. "Marry me baby."

Tears filled my eyes with deep infatuation. I shook my head up and down. "Yes…..yes. I'll marry you."

"Yeah?"

"Yes Thomas. I'll marry you. I wolfve you?" He smiled. Tears filled his eyes.

"I'll be witch you forever. I love you too my love."

He lifted my dress over my head. He trailed his tongue up and down my body. I panted as I watched him lick and suck me all over. He took my breast in his mouth while he fingered my click. Fuck I'm so wet. "You dripping for me love?"

"For you, and you only." He took me in his mouth flickering his tongue up and down my clit.

The electric shocks rocked my body. I grabbed at his head holding his man bun in my grip.

He let me control his head moving it back and forth in the direction of my control. I grinded on his mouth.

When he looked up at me, and I had to watch his grey eyes fixated and his thick tongue going in and out my hole, I fucking lost it. "Yessss....yessss. give me all that come baby. You're so fucking beautiful when you come." I squinted my eyes and moaned so loud.

I'm sure all my guards heard me. I'm sure the animals in the mountains heard me.

My whole body shaked until it passed. And it was fucking amazing. I pointed my finger and beckoned him on top of me.

I kissed all my secretion off his tongue, face, and beard. "Are you sure?" He asked. I unbuckled his pants and helped him out his shirt. His dick is big. Like horse dick big. Like what the fuck, I think I'm gonna back out big. Unhuman. He winked at me when he saw me staring too hard. "Yes. I'm sure."

His tongue was back in my mouth and his hands were gliding across my breast. My nipples were rock hard.

He let spit from his tongue drip down on my nipples and then sucked it up with his mouth. I grabbed his cock in my hands to guide it myself.

Maybe it will hurt less if I put it in. He ran his fingers through my hair before he penetrated me. I sucked in a deep breath at his entry. I was too tight.

He barely was able to get the head of his cock in. "Breathe baby." He said when he saw my panting grew heavier. He went back down and sucked on my pussy. I was begging for his entry. Trying to pull his body up myself. "Please." I begged.

"Please what." He asked taking his tongue out of me momentarily.

"Please come up here and fuck me."

"I don't fuck you. I make love to you. Well for our first time anyway." He smiled.

He started off slowly. I screeched in pain when his entire cock thrusted through my walls. It was so fucking painful. I bit my lip.

He gave me his to bite instead. "Don't hurt yourself, hurt me. Bite me. Hold onto me, scratch my back if you have to." He moaned closing his eyes, enjoying the tight feel of me. I know men like that shit. *What the fuck you do to me.* He muttered in his mind, dropping his head down.

He glided slowly in and out of me. I felt pain with each thrust. I didn't care though. It was pain I was willing to endure for him. He moaned, I moaned.

He went faster and I dug my nails into his back. I started feeling pleasure with the pain.

The pain turned into pleasure after a while. He knew it too. He went faster and harder. He slowed down and made me look at him. "I love you. Your mines. Do you hear me." I shook my head yes. "I'll fucking kill for you. I'll die for you." My pussy got wetter as he said those words while sliding in and out of me.

He's a fucking beast. My beast. My wolf boy. I felt his dick throbbing inside of me. It must have meant he was ready to explode, and since I don't think I can come because of the mixed pleasure and pain. I wanted him to release.

"It's ok baby. You come for me now. I know you want to. You feel all this wet tight pussy wrapped around your big cock. Sliding in and out of me. It's yours baby." He panted heavy as if my words sent a spark through him. He held me at my hips one hand on each side, controlling how hard I slammed against him.

I looked at him pounding away at me. His chest and arm muscles popped out with every thrust he made. I grinded down on him to fuck him back, and he lost his mind. I heard the howl in his chest.

Oh, he was wolf alright. He tilted his head up. "That's right come for me. Come all inside of me baby. I'm yours." He fucking roared like a fucking animal.

His dick throbbed inside of me as I felt his come drip into my walls. Pump, by pump.

I closed my eyes while he came inside of me, and I channeled. It was like I went into another dimension. The sky thundered, the fire burned, the wind warped, the ocean rose.

It was at that moment I realized I came with him, and it was so intense I didn't realize I was screaming with him. My walls held his cock in its grip.

I tightened around him, until I opened my eyes and my climax passed. Then I released him.

He fell beside me on the bed and we both layed on our backs panting like we just ran for miles.

Moments later we finally got up to bathe and then eat the dinner that was now cold. I felt different. My private hurted when I sat down, that's for sure.

That's not the different I felt though. I felt like a woman. As we ate, all he did was stare at me.

It was kind of awkward. His stare was similar to a territorial dominance. I

knew he would never let me out of his sight. And that's terrible, because my heart is bleeding for Lee. What the fuck did I just do.

The sex was amazing. Well for what I assume amazing can be. He was my first, but I didn't feel a spark in my spirit like I thought I would.

I can't explain it, but I know what I'm talking about. It certainly doesn't help that I just agreed to marry him, let him court me, and still, I think of another.

My fucking heart plays too many games with me.

What the hell do I do now.

THIRTY

KATIANNA

The year was going by the longest it's ever been. Maybe because I endured and took on so much in a short period of time.

It's amazing how one day you're just a child looking to go outside and play with your friends, and within the blink of an eye, you're an adult with way more responsibilities than you asked for.

Sometimes, some of us grow up overnight. That is certainly the background of my story. Now, there's no going back. Life begins.

I've learned a lot about myself in these past few months. Losing my mother and losing Stacey was a huge setback for me.

I became an angry person, I became lost. I became cold hearted. My mother always taught me to lead with the people's best interest.

Father taught me to lead with my heart. I choose to lead with my soul. It speaks to me. I'm still learning how to listen to it, but it speaks to me loud and clear. I certainly suffer the consequences for the actions I take when I don't listen to my soul.

The *Blackfield* festival is approaching. I'm nervous more than ever. Having to see former interests will be no walk in the park for me. I wish them all well. I certainly hope they're happy.

For now, I continue to be the fairest leader I can be. I've already made so many changes.

Layla, Rebecca, and Victoria screamed for me from the windows. I was surprised to see Victoria. She just got married to a fine fellow named Riddick. I was so happy for her. She's with child.

"Come down." The girls yelled.

I ran like a little girl. I was excited at nothing and everything. Those girls brung out the child in me. Even Layla. I was panting running down the spiral staircase to get to them. Once outside I seen them holding hands staring at me all weird.

"Go on, what is it?" Allison popped out of the blue moon sky. They held out huge sign. I ran into their arms once I read it. They are truly the most thoughtful girls I've ever met. Sometimes I feel guilty for liking them too much.

We took each other arm and arm and danced right there in the middle of the commonms. No music, no audience, just us.

That was enough fun with the girls. I had a meeting with Black Village over their months short supply. I was hoping James had nothing to do with this.

It had seemed as though they shorted us of supplies once James went back to his Village.

He promised me he'd never trade on me or treat me any differently. We'll see once I see him. I reached out once. I wrote a letter wishing him well.

My letter was returned. I was told he specifically refused it. Victoria gets information from her new husband when they pillow talk.

Riddick was of Black Village. Him and Victoria met a few months ago when he came here to trade. They've been inseparable ever since. I had to house him.

It was either Victoria moved there, or he moved here. I selfishly was not willing to let my friend go. So, he's Blue now.

The rule states that one can trade, move, inhabit temporarily in other Villages as long as its leader allows. I signed off on their marriage, and so did Blacks leader.

Mr. Punic sat in his favorite chair as always. The one that faced me directly. He loved looking at me, and not in admiration. He loved reading my facial expressions, he loved judging me.

"We were shorted of supplies that we paid for. What is the reason?"

Their leader explained that it was because they were short on their shipment. He promised we'd get a delivery by the end of the week.

"You came all this way to say something you could sent a letter by traveler." I raised suspension. "What are you doing here Erik?"

"You always were more meticulous than your mother."

I could feel my fire. I had my issues with my mother, but I hated anyone else speaking of her. In any kind of way.

"Apologies, have I offended?"

"What do you want Erik?"

"I want to make a deal."

"And why would we do that. You already owe us a delivery."

"Because I have a piece of information you want."

"Which is?"

"You're good friend Stacey. She's alive and well. She was never murdered. She was taken away and held prisoner."

I channeled immediately. Wrapping the air around his throat.

"You better speak, and you better speak quick." Fire set in my eyes. He choked the tighter my grip became around his neck. I had to release him if I were to hear what he had to say.

He coughed up blood. "As I was saying. I got a valuable piece of information on her whereabouts."

"How do you know this. Where...How." I stuttered for words.

"Did you or anyone ever see a body? Was she ever buried, or were you just told?'

Panic took over as I searched my memory. I closed my eyes and went back to the day I found out. The day Lee told me when he waited in front of my Chambers. He never said what happened to her. He just said she was killed. There was so much going on back then. I didn't think twice about her body. I assumed it was burned to ash like the others.

"What do you want?" I want Black to have first Dibbs on all trades. I want one of your ladies for my son, and I want you to re consider your title. I have a someone in mind who I'd like to take over Blue."

"You're a fool if you think I will give you such ridiculous power for hearsay."

He jumped up out his seat. "Well then I guess she was never that close of a friend." He winked.

I charged at him; his guards fought against my guards to stop me. I was too powerful for every single person in this room.

My soul told me there was truth to his words.

"Wait.....let's talk."

He sat back down, and everyone settled. "As I said. She's alive, and I can take you to her. If my demands are met."

"And who do suppose will rule Blue?"

"James." My heart constricted in my chest at the sound of his name. Was that what this was all about. Was that the reason why he suddenly grew quiet on me. I wondered if any of it was real. Was he ever in love with me or was it all a ploy to take my spot.

"First off. I will NEVER hand over my leadership. Blue is my home. My people. My rule. Second. Your son can have a lady, only if her interests are equal to his. The only thing I can offer is your Village having first Dibbs on all trades."

Erik laughed in my face. All of a sudden Mr. Punic didn't have an opinion. He had everything to say any other time. But now he just sat there like the useless piece of crap that he is. I have no idea why mother had him on the board.

"Now that is not such a good deal for us. We are already high up for trades. Guess you'll have to go on with life without her."

"Or I can kill you where you stand."

"Always ready to kill. I've mistake. You're worse than your mother."

'You're mistaken. I am, and always will be stronger than you."

"You wouldn't want to wage war, now would you? Not after all the piece you've successfully implemented."

Erik and his people walked out. The blood in my veins boiled. My heart was cold in my chest. Probably a block of ice.

If there was one person, I couldn't stand more than anyone else, it was Erik, I never liked him. Every time he came around, he came around he was plotting and scheming.

I always assumed him, and mother was in on things together. I always wondered why my father never said anything about the way them two carried on.

I guess there's a lot I didn't understand about my parents. t's not over though. He may think I will find him and beg him to help me, but I will find out if it's the truth or not. Everything he do, has malicious intent.

It's probably a lie all together. His ploy to overtake my Village. My fucking Village that I worked so hard to mold. My Village where I was born and raises, trained, hurt, bled, cried, lost, won, and had my first kiss.

Erik has no idea that he's playing with fire. I am fire. He's gonna suffer the wrath whether there's truth to his allegations or not.

****

Water dripped as I layed on my bed thinking about what happened in the meeting. My mind ping ponged with the thought of Stacey being alive. I wish it to be the truth.

To save her and have her back at my side would bring me such fortune. To have at least one of the most important persons in my life, back, will solidify everything that hurts me.

I spoke with Lee about it. He said he too, only heard of her death. He never seen an actual body. He assumed what I assumed, that she was ash.

He promised me he'll find the two guards where he got this information from, question them himself, and then bring them to me. Those poor men.

Death becomes them. If Lee has to bring them to me, it meant he suspects them of lying. Then they will be nothing but ash.

Parliament was no help. Mr. Punic refused to send funding for a search and possible rescue.

He had the nerves to look me in my face and tell me, looking for her, was looking for the ghost of no one. He regretted saying that the moment the words left his fat lips.

He'll spend the rest of his day rising in pain. She was worth every penny, even if it meant the rest of us suffer.

I don't even want to think about the fact that James is looking suspicious on top of all this. I wonder if it was his choice, or their choice.

I haven't a clue why I'm being tested. Maybe I'm too nice a leader that people think they can test me. It was time for a change. Time for examples.

Black Village was fancier than ours. Their pillars were made of crystals, sparkling at every eye's angel. Its sparkles followed you like a painting. Like the sun everywhere you go.

My presence tensed the people of this Village. I can see the fear in their eyes, and the whispers in the halls as I bum rushed my way through their gates.

I didn't need guards; I didn't even need permission. All I needed was a little power. Erik jumped out his seat at the sight of me, but I froze his ass down before he could do anything.

His guards jumped, but I froze them too. I'll freeze everybody in this entire Village if I must. If everyone else is playing dirty, then I have no plans to play fair.

All I wanted was peace, but if problems are what everyone wants, then it's what they will receive. I asked for treaties to spear their blood, not mines.

"Now. I will talk, and since your helpless bodies can do nothing but listen. Then listen. I've come for information regarding one of my lady's, and you know exactly what I'm talking about.

You will receive nothing in return for this information, except the air I'm going to allow you to breathe in your lungs.

I'm going to release Erik to talk, and if I even sense that you will do something that's going to irritate me. I will kill you." I smiled as I tilted my head.

Erik gagged on his own spit when I released him. He gasped for him.

"You are mad. You come to my home unannounced demanding favors with no rewards, and you think it will be as simple as the Village you hell from." He spit on the ground. Staring at me with hungry eyes.

"I'd advise you to reconsider."

He channeled his powers, and it was as quick as it was stupid. I dusted that mother fucker to ashes. In my defense, he channeled, and that was an immediate threat to my life.

The frozen Villagers couldn't move or talk, but I sensed with my spirit how shocked, afraid, and angry they were.

"Now. That is mistake number one. Anyone want to be mistake number two." I knew it was rhetorical asking because they couldn't physically, but I wanted them to sense fear.

"I'm going to unfreeze all of you, and if no one tells me what I want to hear, then death be to you all."

"You know you can't do that." A familiar voice crept in the back of my ears. James was nearing. I could feel his gaze at my back.

"Oh look. It's James. Now you can lead your own Village instead of trying to take my spot at mines." I pointed aimlessly at the pile of ash that was once their leader.

"Katianna, I cannot save you from this. This is wrong."

"Save me. Ha. Your hilarious." I tilted my head at him now. "Do I look like I need saving." I furrowed my eyebrows.

"After what you just did. I would say so. Your powers are more powerful than the law."

"I. Am. The. Law."

"Ah ha. I see. What happened the girl who wanted nothing but peace, the girl who wanted nothing but love."

"She's long gone. Replaced with the women who got led astray by a man who tricked her into feelings."

"I did not lead you astray. My feelings for you were real. Is real. Still. Please let's go somewhere and talk."

My better judgement got the best of me. "Ok, but no one will be released until I say so."

He put his hands up in defeat.

When we reached a private sector, he rolled his head around his shoulders as if the only thing he could use right now was a massage.

"Katianna. I was real. We were real."

"Then why has Erik asked me to give up my Village to you."

"I never asked him to do that. He proposed it to me days ago and I respectfully declined. He called me weak and said I was a fool in love for a girl I could never have. I swear it."

"And the refusal of my letter?"

He shook his head up and down. "Now that was all me. I was hurt. I was bitter. I had heard you were happy with your lover, and the thought of another man touching you turned my stomach.

That kiss we had under the stars, felt beyond this world. The letter we exchanged." He pulled the envelope from his pockets. Showing me that he clearly walks around with it. "That letter means more to me than you'll ever know or understand. So yes, I refused your letter. I thought it be best I cut you out my heart completely, because there's no way we can just be friends."

His confession sent shock waves through my body. I was speechless. I knew he was telling the truth.

"I'm sorry if I hurt you. What we shared was real. All I wanted was to know if you were ok. There will always be a piece of me that cares for you. Your nothing someone I want to simply forget. I held you to your promises. You promised me you'll always be there."

"And I always will." He stood up and walked to me, placing his hand on mine. "I always will, but just not the way you want it."

"Erik told me he had information about a close friend of mine. Who was believed to be killed when my Village was attack. He told me she's held up somewhere and that he would help me find her if I gave into his demands, However, I don't do demands."

"I have no knowledge of this, I assure you. But I will ask around. Now can you please unfreeze my people before they die. Bad enough we have a funeral without a body to plan."

"Of course." I rose from my chair.

"Power looks good on you by the way." He winked. I smiled.

"He'll return in one hour." I told James as I walked off. He stood there confused, but I had no time to explain.

I've discovered a magnificent power during these months of darkness. If I turn someone to ash, and reveres the ash within an hour of burning, they can return in human form.

Alive again, like they never left. I found out there was truth to Willows and David's allegations. I'm starting to really enjoy the witch in me.

I unfroze his people and reversed the ash. They stood around dazed. No one spoke a word. They all watched my back as I glided towards the door skipping like it was the happiest day of my life.

THIRTY-ONE

KATIANNA

Days passed and there was no word on Stacey. I will never give up on finding out if she's still alive. I've had plenty leads.

I've used most of our resources on finding answers. We've come up short every time.

Erik was summoned to my Court where he gave up the information he was told. It led to nothing. Perhaps his reliable resource wasn't so reliable.

The two guards who told Lee of their findings was sure they saw her dead body before she was burned alive.

They even described what she was wearing. Which was true to details. They described her wearing her favorite pink dress with tiny white flowers flooded on the hem. There was no way it was a lie.

My heart bled a second time for her. Not finding answers felt like her death was new news all over again. False hope was the worst kind of hope. Maybe mother was right. Hope was an excuse for failure.

****

Thomas rubbed my feet as I bathed. I like the little things he does for love. I hadn't told him I have no plans on marrying him. I know he's growing suspicious.

I haven't let him touch me intimately since the first time. Every time he tries, I make up excuses as to why I can't. It was either my stomach hurted, I was bleeding, my head hurted, my back hurted, or I was too tired.

I knew it was wrong to be leading him on thus far, but it isn't like I hate him. I still have feelings for him, it's just not in the same way he has for me.
"When will we set a date for the wedding?"

I gulped in my throat. "There's no rush, I want you to focus on the rebuilding of Grey."

"You were so eager to choose me just days ago, and now you pretend like it's the last thing from your mind. Please tell me what's happened?"

My foot slipped from his hands, causing my body to shift underneath. Water splashed outside the tub. "Sorry. I didn't mean to let your foot slip." He regained my foot in his hand. I pulled it away. I knew what was coming. "Please tell me. Do you still love me?"

"Of course, I do." It wasn't a lie. I do love him. "I just don't feel the need to rush. You have a lot going on. I have a lot going on, and we still have to figure out what the arrangements will be when your Village stands."

He walked to the bed and sat down. "I found him." He spoke it so normal as if I were to understand what he was talking about. "The man who saved me when I was a child. The man who gave the "all clear" when I hid in the closet. The man with the scar."

I nearly fell to the ground when I jumped out the tub naked. His eyes scanned my naked wet body. I wrapped myself with a towel and sat beside him. "Oh Thomas. I'm glad you have. Where did you find him....I mean how."

"Right here in Blue Village. He's one of your Villagers. I jumped back.
"Impossible. My mother. My.."

"It's true. I laid my eyes on him for the first time today. He was pushing wheel barrels up the hill, and into the train zone. I'll never forget his face. It was him, I'm sure of it. He looks the exact same, only older."

"But that would mean blue."

"That's exactly what it means. Blue is responsible to the death of my Village." He stared blank in space. "All my life I looked for that man. I wondered what I would do or how I would feel if I ever saw him again, and now……and now boom."

"Thomas, I'm sorry. I assure I had no idea Blue was responsible for the loss of your Village." My heart cried for his. I felt so bad. If there was any truth to this, then I'd be ashamed.

"Maybe it was treaty gone wrong. Maybe it was a million other reasons, but Katianna, your mother caused my families death." Tears centered his eyes. He was hurting. And there was nothing I could do about it."

"I don't blame you. But I do blame your mother. It was during her reign. The revenge I feel seeping into my wolf fights with the love and respect I have for you. Because even though being here will never feel right, my heart still belongs to its leader. And I'm still here wanting to marry and protect you."

There were no words. There was no action. It's not like I can summon the man he speaks of. It's not like I will go against my own people. It's not like my sympathy will suddenly dissipate his feelings.

I dropped my towel letting him look at me. It was the only thing I could do.

My nipples hardened from the cold air, and he surely seized the moment. He took my breast in his mouth, and I allowed him the pleasure.

Even though I wasn't in it. I was in it. I closed my eyes while he pounded into me. He fucked me angry. And I took the pain for him.

There was no sensual kissing and touching. Not much fourplay besides my breasts. It was a pure hatred fuck. He needed this. It was the least I could do.

"I'm in love with you. Marry me." He muttered as he came.

"Ok. I'll marry you." I would have told him anything to calm my wolf boy down. I'll do anything to save my people. If I had said no, I was sure there would be blood on a wolfs fangs.

He touched me all night.

"I hope you get pregnant." He said as he rolled over to his normal sleeping position.

He doesn't even go home anymore. He shares my bed every night, and leaves in the morning. I'm so screwed. I guess I have a weeding to plan.

I guess mother was right. Matters of the heart doesn't matter at all. I'm doing exactly what she said I should do. What's best for my Village. He's a leader. He's gifted. His Village will become my Village. A guaranteed alliance. *I'm so sorry Lee. You will always have my armor; you will always have my real heart.*

THIRTY-TWO
THOMAS

After everything I've done for her. After everything we went through, this is the thanks I get. I do everything I can to show her how much I love her.

To show her how appreciative I am that she chose me. I can tell that something has shifted in her feelings towards me. She won't let me touch her.

I try to get her to open up to me, and she shoots me down. I'm surprised she agreed to marry me after having to ask her a second time.

She wore the ring I made for her, but she'd take it off whenever she knew she was gonna cross paths with Lee. I don't hate the guy.

I know they have childhood history, but I wish I left him to die back on the front lines of the last war. I saved him because of who he is to her.

I'm surely regretting that now. I will not take credit for who've she become, but I helped trained her. She begged me to come back to Blue with her.

I was fine in the woods by myself. She won't set a date for the wedding, yet she's so wrapped up in the festival that's coming up.

Why can't she realize she literally mean the world to me. If she or her little powerless commoner boy thinks that I'm going to simply vanish into Grey Village, then they both have another thing coming.

My wolf imprinted on her. That means I have to protect her forever, no matter what. She might as well be mines.

I'm willing to do anything to make her fall for me again. Including pardoning the man I want to kill with my bare hands.

I found the guy who saved me as a kid. The one with the scar. I finally found him, and although he spared me that day.

Him and this entire fucking Blue Village is responsible for my family's death. Responsible for the entire wipe-out of my Village.

However, I love Katianna more than I want revenge. But she's making it hard.

When I look in her eyes, all I want to do is tell her my secrets. Tell her that I wasn't exactly truthful.

Every time I try to have a heart to heart with her, she tenses up and push me away. I don't know what else to do. I'll die fighting for her love though.

THIRTY-THREE

LEE

She hurt me, but I love her. I wish I didn't. I wish I could fall in love with someone else. I've had women beg me. Treat me with respect, and still I wanted her. But she chose him.

She doesn't know I digged dirt on him. I didn't tell her because I wanted her decision to be based off true love. Not information. She came back one night with a ring on her finger.

I wanted to take his head. I knew he had her. Courted her. Touched the women I love more than he. I was sick to my stomach.

It won't last when she finds out what I know. But at least no one could ever say I stepped on their toes to get the girl, and when it blows up in her face, she better not come running to my arms.

I won't be there to hold her this time.

****

Five months later

The doors to my Chambers swung open. My heart danced in my chest. It took a long time for me to get over the pain I felt, but I did.

"You look beautiful Ms. Chatman." My wife spun around. I got married two months ago.

Love finally found me. And it feels so fucking good. I feel like a new man. I now had a family of my own to protect.

Especially being that Allison was finally here. Keeping her out of trouble is no easy task. Keeping her and Katianna apart was an even harder task.

They were thick as thieves. The best of friends. Sure, they had their fair share of arguments over me, but Allison always loved Kati, they were always like sisters. I'm happy no wedge formed between them.

She danced towards me and forced me up off my feet to dance with her. How dare I refuse. I was happy if she was happy, no matter what it was.

We danced around like silly children. We even jumped up and down on the bed. That turned into kissing. Kissing turned into touching.

Next thing I know we were making love. Every time we kissed, it led to making love. We could never kiss in public; it was like she could read my mind.

She'd grab me from wherever we were, and we couldn't make it back to the Chambers, we would make love wherever we could. In dark corners, I'd bend her over. In the kitchen. Even in the woods when we had dates.

We've been caught multiple times, and we've been complained about multiple times, but we didn't care. We always laughed and ran.

"I have to go husband." She giggled under the covers. Then wrapping herself up in the covers as she spun herself into it. Leaving me out cold and naked. She laughed as she ran off to the bath. I chased behind her. I love how we're so playful.

"No. Seriously I must go. I am charge of costume for the **Blackfield Festival**."

"Ok fine but be back in time. We have plans." Pop. I slapped her ass. My wife has the finest ass.

I can't believe it's almost time for the festival again. Thank God all the Villages are at peace for now.

After the last war we had, there was no telling how things were going to play out. I'm just happy to be in love with somebody that loves me back. Finally.

When my wife returned to our Chambers, we left out for dinner. She promised me that one day a week will be dedicated to me, just us.

So far, she's kept on her promise. She's wearing a green dress, it's her favorite color. She's stunning.

I've seen her dressed up before, but for some reason, tonight, she looks exotic and exquisite. All I want is to take her, right here, on this glass table.

She's so lucky there are people here serving us. She called the kitchen boy to her side, and he gathered the staff and ran off.

'Thank God. I wanted to be alone with you."

Bad idea. If we're alone, I'm going to take you.

The slit on her green dress rose as she extended her leg. She knew I was looking. She bit her lip. She knows what that does to me.

I slid her chair next to mines so she could hear me well. "You're going to have to stop biting your lip, clinching your thighs together, and showing me skin, if you don't want me to take you on this table."

She tilted her head at me. "Why do you think I dismissed them." I quickly rose to my feet picking her up out of her chair, placing her down on her ass.

Lifting her dress was easy. The slit from her thigh down her leg helped me quite a bit. I loosened the tie I wore and unbuttoned the top of my shirt.

Spread her legs open and dropped to my knees to please my pretty kitty. I sucked on her pussy until she begged me to put it in.

I knocked all the shit off the table and propped her further back than the edge she was on. My pants were at my ankles as I thrusted inside of her.

The lights around us flickered off and on. We were so lost in each other.

When she came all over my cock, she jumped down. I was confused at first, until she dropped to her knees and started sucking on my cock.

She never done that before. I threw my head back as I lost my speech. I had zero control. It felt so fucking good having her tongue wrapped around me.

I pulled her up and bent her over the table, taking her from the back. Watching her surrender to me like this was the sexiest shit I ever seen.

Her ass pounced off me every thrust. Her face glided up and down the glass table. I fucked her hard until I exploded inside of her.

We gathered ourselves and sat back down. Only there was no more dinner. Everything was scattered across the floor. I guess she gave them a set time to go missing, because the staff started arriving back.

Their wandering eyes told us everything we already knew. We lost control and they had to clean up the mess we made. She cleared her throat. "I'll have a glass of wine please." The poor kitchen boy was embarrassed. We laughed so hard. God, I love her.

****

The next morning, I woke up in a sweat. It happened sometimes. Seems to be happening more often than not now.

My wife woke me up from my sleep. "Baby, you had a bad dream again." She swiped the sweat off my forehead. "Was it the same nightmare? The one with the girl?"

"Yes." I shook my head. I told her about my bad dreams. It started when I wed my wife. I didn't have the heart to tell her that because I didn't want her to think it was related to her. Because it's not.

There was a girl I kept seeing when we went on search for Katianna. She kept popping up out of nowhere.

She was the one who led me to her in the end. It's how I found her and Thomas. I'll never forget the last thing the little girl said to me. "My journey ends where your destiny begins."

I play that line over and over in my head. Wondering if she's come back. If she was trying to give me a message.

In my dreams, she pops up looking raggedy like she did in real time. She keeps telling me that someone's in trouble come quick.

I take her hand and she leads me straight off a cliff into the ocean, and she disappears when we fall, but I hit the water and fight for my life.

I wake up out my sleep every time at the same part. The part where I almost drown to death.

"Maybe we should have some people look around. See if she's nearby." My wife suggested.

"Yeah. Maybe."

Allison burst into our Chambers and jumped in our bed. Helping herself to my side of the pillows. "Hello family." She smiled.

"One day, you're going to catch your brother and I making love and it'll be stuck in your head forever."

"Oh, you mean like how everyone else in Village have caught you two perverts."

"Shut up."

They began pillow fighting and I excused myself to a bath.

It was nice seeing how close they've become.

The next few days were a blur. I spent all the free time I had searching for answers on the missing girl. No one in Village reported seeing her. I had forgotten all about her until I started having those dreams.

I requested a search and rescue for Sir Ranald. One of my men that was left ill back in White Village.

When Jackson, former leader of White came for his daughters hearing. I asked him about my man. He grew angry and told me he wanted to stay in White.

He said he was there at his own will. I knew it was bullshit. I should have acted sooner. I would have, had it not been for war, passion, hurt, and everything in between that deterred my attention. But that was then, and this is now. I needed answers.

My wife is not too happy about my abrupt trip, but she understands.

We sailed off in two boats. Upon arriving. The place looked weirder than it did the last time I was here.

"State your business here." Willow immediately denied me entry.

"I've come for a friend. His name is Ross. He was left here months ago. He was ill. I had your father's word that he'd return when he was able. Only he never turned up."

"There is no such man here Lee of Blue. Last time you were here. You snaked your way around pretending to be one of us. Tricking ladies into love for information.

Why should we trust you or help you?" Lily stood at her side with her face frowned.

"Because you're breathing for starters. And I'm the reason for that. Do you know how hard it was to talk Blues Village leader out of taking your head." I smirked. "You know and I know, what Katianna is capable of. She gave you a second chance. So, you're going to let us in, or I will go back to her and tell her what's happened here." Fear seeped into their eyes as they stood aside to let us through. It wasn't the warm welcoming I expected but it was one none-the-less.

We searched around util we found him. He was alive and well. Looks like he was well fed.

"Ross." I grabbed to hug him. He grabbed me back. "Boys." He shouted. He reeked of alcohol. He stumbled like he was drunk.

The woman occupying his company told us that he was always drunk. We nearly had to carry him back to the boat. He spoke in a weird tongue when we dropped his body to the ships ground. It was the same weird tongue they all spoke when I last visited.

"We'll get him sobered up and tomorrow we'll find the truth." I said to Nigel, who was closer to him.

****

Tomorrow never came. Not for him anyways. He passed in his sleep last night. Of course, I knew there had to be something else going on.

I'd launch an investigation. Maybe he was poisoned. For now, I had to focus on my new bride, who I hadn't seen all night, and all day today. She was so into her role as the head of Costumes for The Blackfield Festival.

I draped my arms around her waist from behind. She folded into me. I felt the weight of nothing fall against me. She smells like fresh flowers and honey. She tasted like it too. I guess it was her natural scent.

"Are you ok my love?"

"I'm fine honey. I felt a little sick this morning, but it's ok."

"Awe. 'm sorry I wasn't there to make you feel better."

I spun her around in a dance. "It's fine. I promise. I'm ok."

My wife always put on a brave face. Everything can go to shit, but she'll still put on a brave face.

"I just want everything to be perfect for the festival."

"And it will be if you have anything to do with it."

She smiled as we swayed in each other's arms.

"I'm sorry about your friend." She tightened her hands on my arms. Anyone that knew me knows, Ross was a close friend of mine.

The day we shipped out to search for Katianna, I promised his wife and son that I'd bring him back in one piece.

I looked his son in his eyes and promised him he'll see his father again and can play all the kickball he wanted with him.

Ross's wife died when the Village was attacked. Leaving Rue parentless. That poor kid hated me for a long time when I showed back up to Village.

I had thought his father returned long before me. Sadly, that was not the case. I then promised him I'd find his father and bring him back.

It was a hope I hoped would hope. When I visited Rue last night and told him the good news about his father.

His eyes filled with tears, and he hugged onto my legs begging to see him. I told him he had to rest for the night and that he would see him tomorrow.

I will never forget the look in his eyes when I broke to news to him this afternoon of his father's death. He began hitting me with all the might his little balled up fist could produce.

He screamed over ten times how much he hated me and hoped I died. It broke my heart. I've felt sorrow before, but never like this. My wife agreed that we'd take him in as our own. I swear she's the sweetest toughest girl I know.

THIRTY-FOUR

KATIANNA

Seven Months Later

After all that's happened. I can't help the pull I've always felt in my heart. I'd always known it would be him. No matter how much I tried to deny it. I knew it. From the moment he walked into my life. My soul connected to his like no other.

I wondered why my heart fluttered differently at the sight of him. All the tricks my heart played on me. I finally figured her out.

****

He sat with his back turned. I crept slowly tiptoed. When I neared him, he reached his arms behind his back and grabbed me. Pulling me onto his lap. "How'd you know it was me?" I asked.

"Your scent is like no other. I will always know when it is you." He planted a kiss on my forehead. Then a kiss to my growing belly.

"You're even more beautiful carrying our child." His gaze locked on mines. We interlocked our hands together as I rested my head on his shoulder. "I cannot wait to meet our son." He said while rubbing my stomach. "Or our daughter." I countered.

"Right or our daughter. Either way. I will love our child and give you both the best of me. And if it is a daughter, my only wish is that she is just as strong, smart, challenging, and as pretty as her mother."

"If it is a boy, I pray that he is as charming, skillful, handsome, and as hardheaded as his father." We both laughed.

"Katianna." He called to me. I lifted my head to his gaze. "Thank you for choosing me." A look of complete and utter infatuation spread across his face. I drew in a breath.

"You were always the only choice. Because I didn't choose. My soul chose yours, and that's more powerful than love. I love you more than love." I traced the outline of his heart with a heart. I remembered when he said it to me the day, they all went off to fight on the front lines.

We stayed there. No more words were spoken. We listened to each other breathe. Watching the sunset fall behind the mountains.

It was the first time we were ever this quiet for this long. The most precious silence I ever stood in. In two months, we'll be parents.

Neither of us with a clue as what to do to prepare. But I've never felt more ready about something in my life than I do about becoming a mother.

He doesn't know this, but I know it's a girl and a boy. Twins. My gift told me so, and I could feel two heartbeats. I should know.

I'm being kicked everyday by four feet. It's as if they're fighting for space.

Bickering siblings already.

Hold on my babies, you soon come.

You are all invited to the ceremony for:

The Welcoming of New Life

Your Village leader: Lady Katianna

&

Her Husband: Sir Lee Chatman

Celebrate with them as they bring the royal baby and your future leader into life. WE ARE BLUE. WE ARE PROUD. BABY BLUE ON THE WAY.

THIRTY-FIVE

KATIANNA

Two truths and a lie

1. I once stabbed a stuffed animal to death.

2. I jumped off cliffs as a kid.

3. I'm a witch.

>Letter to my younger self:

Dear Katianna,

>You've made it this far. One day you will wake
>>up and things are going to be different for you.
>>>Don't feel defeated. Don't run. It's going to be
>>>>ok. The world is not ready to receive you yet, but
>>>>>they will. You're going to go on a really cool date,
>>>>>>with a cool guy. It's where you're going to

be writing this letter. You will face many Challenges, and you will overcome each one. So, breathe, laugh, love. Win. Fail. Cherish.

EPILOGUE

I was happy it was all over. The only War I want to wage, is the one in my heart. When Lee gave me the information he had on Thomas. I didn't believe it.

When it was confirmed. My heart broke into a million sliver pieces. I couldn't believe the man I had chosen was capable of the things I heard.

There was a part of me that was relieved. I really didn't want to marry him, and Lee gave me a way out. I was hurt, but I knew deep down that he wasn't the one.

I felt foolish not picking Lee in the first place, like I knew should have. Him forgiving me and taking me back, was a debt I could never repay. I

t took a while for him to get over the fact that I once, even if it was just briefly, belonged to another.

Him looking at our twins in their basins is the best thing I'll ever witness. He loves them so much. He never once questioned if they were his or not. It didn't matter. We were together within one week after my split with Thomas.

We were intimate days after that. I felt shame having taken two men in bed within one month of each other, but my children are here now.

Lee is my husband, and we are a family. Childbirth was rough. I nearly survived it. Our daughter's name is Stacey-Ann, and our sons, Peter. Named after Lees father.

Lees father had come back to Village after spending years in Denmark with Allison.

He was killed shortly after his return. Lee took it hard. Allison took it harder. I spent my days delaying my duties while I cared for them both.

Thomas was responsible for Lees father death. He killed him after he learned that he was the man with the scar. The man that spared him in the closet.

Thomas had promised me as long as he had me. He'd seek no justice. That was clearly a lie to take me in bed once more.

I think he knew I no longer had romantic feelings for him. Things got worse when Lee found out.

When he was a boy and channeled his wolf for the first time. He killed many children in Blue Village. It was before my mother waged war.

Greys Village leader Armond, (Thomas's father) ordered a hit on my mother's head. That's what led to the fall out.

Lee and Thomas battled in the fields just outside the gates. When Thomas channeled his wolf to attack Lee, I had no choice but to kill him.

It was the saddest thing I had to do. I twisted his wolf in vines I used when I channeled earth. Grey wheezed until it broke his bones.

It was the saddest thing I ever had to do. Kill Grey after he'd protected so many times before.

I finished him with fire. It was the quickest kill I could think of. I wanted it so badly to be over.

I cried for days, and Lee was right there by my side. Wiping the tears away. I didn't deserve him.

****

The *Blackfield festival* was a huge success. Rebecca got the golden rose and dinner invitation from the winner of Jousting.

Lady Amanda was the chosen hand in marriage. Seeing T-B-N was hard for me, but time has passed, and we've become good friends. I convinced The Gods to gift him leadership of Grey Village.

He graciously accepted. He's my fire breathing dragon boy.

New era, new set of powers, new rules, and new beginnings. I finally felt free. I was finally happy.

Looking at my babies was worth every bit of misery and pain I suffered, and I'd do it all over again if it meant that I'd still get to have them in the end.

They are identical twins. I have a rough time telling them apart. If it wasn't for me being able to look at their privates to know who was who, I'd be lost.

Lee, on the other hand, knows our children like the back of his hand. I know in my soul that they are his. They both favor him so much. They have his nose. They have his blue eyes.

I feel so protective and loving of the twins. I can't understand how me, and my mother wind up have the relationship we had.

I can't picture myself being mean to my children. I will never want them having to grow up questioning if I love them, or if they were good enough.

That will mess up a child's mind. It certainly played with mines. Even now, as a grown woman, I yearn for her approval. It's something that will never go away, and it's something that I'll never receive.

She may have told me sweet nothings on her death bed, but that will never amount to the years she missed showing me. Words means nothing without action, and dreams mean nothing without its chaser. My children will dream big.

Lee walked to me, placing a kiss on my forehead. He was still so in love with me still. I love him for that. He still showed me equally amount of attention, as he did the twins. I'll never forget when I gave birth, the look on his face when a second baby popped out.

"I hope you're proud of me momma." I said into the sky. Air swept across my face. I knew she was proud. Lee held my hand and rubbed my back. He's all I need. He's all I ever needed.

ACKNOWLEDGMENTS

It's been a rollercoaster for me releasing this book. This is the first book I ever published. Book one in To Wage War series. So many late nights/early mornings. I even spent fourteen hours straight writing the last pages, getting it ready for the release date. Combing over every little detail to perfection. Only there's no such thing as perfection as we all know. However, I hope that my readers enjoy reading it, as much as I enjoyed writing it. This book started out as a project I started five months ago. There were so many times, I wanted to give up. My love for literature kept me going. I would like to acknowledge all those who played a part in helping to make this possible. My children especially, who took a back seat to my writing, having to miss the attention of their mom so that I could write To Wage War. So many quick dinner nights, get out my room I'm focusing, along with many other things. They were patient. To my friends who helped read some of the chapters, encouraging me to continue writing. I love you all. Look out for To Wage War (Beginning Days.) The story doesn't end until you know where it begins.

Made in the USA
Middletown, DE
14 April 2024